Critical acclaim for D

'Without labouring it, Thorn. ...aliusnes the pervasive solitude of urban life, a state kept at bay with a few habitual friends or by the delayed unravelling of manifestly unsatisfactory relationships . . . Thorne, who is only in his mid-twenties, can write with unfussy ease, and knows how to underplay a joke . . . Readers who might normally prefer to be at the cinema will find this novel an enjoyable experience' *Times Literary Supplement*

'[Thorne] is a talented, ambitious writer . . . you have to admire him' *Time Out*

'From the schmaltzy standpoint of *Sleepless in Seattle*, to the overindulgence of Eighties classics such as *Pretty in Pink* or *The Breakfast Club*, *Dreaming of Strangers* uses its chosen medium in the same way *Our Friends in the North* and *This Life* used their soundtracks to become a *thirtysomething* for the cinema-obsessed' *Hotdog*

Matt Thorne was born in 1974. He is the author of *Tourist* (1998), *Eight Minutes Idle* (Winner of an Encore Award, 1999) and *Dreaming of Strangers* (2000). He also co-edited the recent anthology *All Hail the New Puritans* (2000).

Dreaming of Strangers

MATT THORNE

PHŒNIX

A PHOENIX PAPERBACK

First published in Great Britain in 2000
by Weidenfeld & Nicolson
This paperback edition published in 2001
by Phoenix,
an imprint of Orion Books Ltd,
Orion House, 5 Upper St Martin's Lane,
London WC2H 9EA

A CIP catalogue record for this book
is available from the British Library.

ISBN 0 75381 132 4

Printed and bound in Great Britain by
Clays Ltd, St Ives plc

For My Mother

The fourth flat that morning looked like a cell in a maximum-security prison. Picking up a metal cup and running it across the barred window, Chris said,

'I'm not sure. I really feel I need a shower and a fridge.'

Jessica turned over a page on her clipboard.

'I have a place with a bath.'

'Close enough.'

They walked down to the car. Jessica drove Chris to the next flat.

'The current tenant hasn't moved out yet, but I think you get the general idea.'

Jessica and Chris had built up a tentative friendship over the last few days of warped wainscoting, water-stained ceilings and mildewed carpets. Jessica had confided early on that she hated showing flats that hadn't been emptied, but Chris liked knowing who'd had a place before him. He'd already nearly moved into a flat because there was a *Rumble Fish* postcard on the fridge so when he noticed a framed *Drugstore Cowboy* poster on the bedroom wall it immediately struck him as a good omen.

'You can keep that if you want. It belongs to the landlady.'

'Really?' he asked, looking at her. 'Why does she leave it here?'

'Let's just say she's a very mysterious woman.'

'I see. Well, let's just say I'll take the flat. *Drugstore Cowboy* is one of my favourite films.'

Jessica looked at him, incredulous. 'You're taking this place because of a poster?'

'Looks that way.'

'Don't you want to look at the bathroom?'

He smiled. 'No need. How soon can I move in?'

'He took the place because of the poster?'

Becca made her voice extra-incredulous, knowing Jessica found this sort of quirkiness impossibly entertaining. Being taken seriously swelled her friend with excitement, and she sounded almost giddy as she added,

'He talked about some other film as well.'

'What film?'

'I can't remember.'

Becca watched her sip her coffee. She wasn't going to press further. Then she noticed the smile at the corner of Jessica's lips.

'Oh, you know you do this just to torment me. Who was in it?'

'Steve Martin. It was some Steve Martin film.'

'*The Jerk*? *The Man with Two Brains*?'

'No, neither of them.'

'Something more recent? *Bowfinger*?'

'Oh, I don't remember, Becca. It had *guy* in the title. The something guy.'

'*The Lonely Guy*,' said Becca, sitting back with a satisfied smile. 'What did he say about it?'

Jessica's bracelets slid down her wrists as she put her elbows up on the table.

'He was talking about some bit where Steve Martin goes round looking for apartments.'

'Is this guy a writer then?'

'What makes you ask that?'

'That's the part Steve Martin plays. A writer who gets dumped by his girlfriend.'

'Yeah, I think he does something like that. It's more journalism though. But not for anyone in particular. I mean, he's at home during the day.'

'Attractive?'

'Sort of. He looks a bit like that guy from *The X Files*.'

'David Duchovny.'

'Yeah, except not as sneaky.'

'You think David Duchovny looks sneaky?'

She nodded. 'He looks like his private life might be really disturbing.'

'But this guy doesn't look like that?'

'No, he's got the same sort of colouring but his face is much more open. He's got really nice eyes.'

'David Duchovny,' Becca considered. 'Not really my type. Never mind. Is he going to trash the place?'

'I don't think so. He doesn't look like a party animal.'

'Maybe I should call in. Introduce myself.'

'Maybe you should.'

Becca didn't say anything.

'How are things with James?' Jessica asked.

'OK. It's strange being with someone so normal.'

'But you always hated going out with weirdos.'

'I know,' she sighed, 'but you have to admit it was funny.'

'Are you still in contact with any of those guys?' asked Jessica.

'Are you kidding? God knows what I'd do if one of them showed up now. My life's so . . . different.' She paused. 'What about you? Are you seeing anyone?'

Jessica shook her head. 'I just always think about having to bring them back to my parents' place. I mean, not that they'd mind, but . . .'

'You could always go home with the guy.'

'Mmm, I know.' She looked away. 'The question hasn't come up in a while.'

Becca caught the waiter's eye.

'Another coffee?'

'Sorry, I can't, I'm showing a property at twelve.'

Becca tried not to show her disappointment. Having a long lunch always seemed a good way of breaking up the day, but she'd forgotten how dangerous it was to eat with people who had jobs to get back to. Watching Jessica gather up her belongings reminded her of how much she wanted a new contract, and she just knew there wouldn't be any calls waiting for her when she got home.

'OK. Call me before Sunday.'

Jessica nodded. 'I will.'

Chris watched the crowd. No matter how many Friday nights he spent in this same spot, he knew he'd never get used to the bustle of Leicester Square. He kept seeing faces he thought he recognised, getting so distracted he almost missed Andy's arrival. His friend always showed up like this, face flushed, forehead glossed, talking too fast because he'd come straight from his show.

They put their tickets on Switch and went into the lobby. 'Do you want anything?' Andy asked.

Chris shook his head. There was only a short queue for food, and Chris waited behind Andy. His friend looked back at him.

'So what's Diana doing?' he asked.

'Moving back with her parents,' Chris replied.

'Where is she now?'

'With Annabel.'

'Sounds dangerous.'

'What can she do? It's already over.'

'Still.' He turned to the man in the red uniform waiting to serve him. 'A tray of nachos, please.'

Chris noticed their reflection in the bronzed mirrors behind the escalators. It was always a shock to see himself when he'd been inside all day. He never bothered making an effort for going to the cinema with Andy, and felt embarrassed about the way he looked beside his friend. If Andy was just naturally smart, it wouldn't be so bad, but the extra polish added by his make-up and hair stylists made the contrast between them even more stark.

'Can you hold these a minute?' Andy asked, handing him his plastic tray. 'I just need the toilet.'

'Jesus, Andy, you know those things make me sick.'

'Come on, I don't want to take them in the toilet. I'll only be a second.'

Chris took the tray and smiled at the man ripping tickets. He wandered over to the posters on the wall of the second floor. Sometimes a poster seemed a more reliable friend than a film. Posters showed up months before a movie and stuck around weeks afterwards, often taking on a life of their own. Hell, sometimes they even made someone rent an otherwise ordinary flat. He thought of posters he'd known and loved: the horror-movie holograms, the speaking spacemen, that beautiful Art Deco design for *The Rocketeer*. He liked that one so much he even put a bid in at a charity auction at his local ABC, almost convincing himself that seventy-five pounds on a piece of shaped cardboard was money well spent.

Andy returned from the toilet. They got back on the escalators and continued to the uppermost floor. They entered the auditorium and found two seats. No matter what film they chose it always seemed to be in the smallest screen. Chris scowled as Andy brought out a plastic bottle of Lucozade from his jacket pocket.

'What?' he asked.

'Why do you always have to do that?'

'What?'

'Bring a skanky bottle. Why can't you buy a drink like everybody else?'

'Because I resent paying three pounds fifty for a bucket of watery syrup and some ice.'

'But you've just spent five pounds on nachos.'

'Three. Besides, they don't do Lucozade.'

'That's because Lucozade is fucking disgusting. Put those nachos on your side of the seat.'

Andy went silent for a moment, then said, 'So will you and Diana be in the house together again?'

'Yeah, for a couple of nights.'

'And you're sure there's no chance of a reconciliation?'

'Positive.'

The adverts started. Andy handed Chris the nachos.

'How many times do I have to tell you? Get those fucking things away from me.'

'Hold them for a minute.'

'Why?'

'I need the toilet again.'

'But you only just went.'

'I can't help it. I've been drinking water all day.'

'Leave them on your seat.'

'Someone'll knock them over. Go on, Chris, please.'

Chris sighed and took the plastic tray. He watched Andy disappear up the aisle and then looked round at the audience. He noticed a single woman alone at the end of the row behind him. She was wearing a black top with a straight neckline and had very glossy red hair. Chris thought there was nothing sexier than a woman who came to the cinema alone. He'd never acted on this thought, thinking of the cinema as a private place and finding the idea as inappropriate as sneaking into someone's house to proposition them.

'What trailer did I miss?' Andy asked on his return.

'I can't remember.'

'But you only just saw it.'

'I wasn't concentrating. Something with Samuel L. Jackson.'

Andy took back his nachos and settled into his seat. He kept up a commentary through the remainder of the trailers, only stopping when the BBFC certificate flashed up. It was obvious why Andy was the one with his own cable show. His opinions seemed definitive, and once he'd reviewed a film it was hard for Chris to think of it without remembering what his friend had said. Chris's thoughts on film were far too wayward, and he even found it hard to decide if some films were good or bad. He had little respect for conventional story-telling, preferring dead spots to dramatic sequences. Often while watching a movie he considered making a tape of these moments, stringing them together to show his students what he liked best about films. Chris had lots of ideas like this in the cinema, most of which got left behind when the movie ended.

After the film had finished, they gathered up their stuff and walked back out to the escalators. As they rode down to the ground floor, Chris looked for the red-haired woman, but she'd already gone.

Andy took his mobile from his pocket. 'He should be on his way, but I'll just check.'

Chris nodded. Andy's brother was a taxi driver. He worked for a minicab firm that hardly ever gave him any work, largely because he hadn't shown up for New Year's Eve two years before, or so he claimed. Consequently, he was almost always available to pick up Chris and Andy, ferrying them about for half-fare.

'Alright?' Chris asked, after Andy pocketed his mobile.

Andy nodded. 'He's outside.'

Becca couldn't remember the last time she'd gone to the cinema with James. She had started their relationship assuming it'd be like all her others and that they'd spend Friday or Saturday watching at least one of the new releases. But gradually, over the first few months of their courtship, James had hinted that he found it stressful to get to the cinema after his week's work, and while he didn't mind watching films, he preferred it if they got them from the video shop.

She still went to the cinema, of course, but on her own and during the week. And while she accepted James' tiredness, she wasn't a big fan of their local Blockbuster. James loved it, pleased that they had multiple copies of almost everything he wanted to watch. For James, seeing a film on video wasn't all that different from watching one in the cinema and he saw no distinction between a film viewed on the big screen or at home.

Every trip to the video shop followed the same pattern. James would stride across to the wall of latest titles, picking up three or four new films he'd like to see. Becca would veto his choices, and come back with a handful of straight-to-video tapes that James would refuse on the grounds that:

a) he'd never heard of them.
b) there was no one famous in them. (He didn't count Donald Sutherland or Charlie Sheen as famous.)

and

c) they'd be shit.

While Becca couldn't really argue with the first two points, she was actually a pretty good prospector of video-hell, and on the rare occasions that he let her have her way, he usually agreed she'd made a good choice.

If they got through these stages without either of them giving in (this usually depended on what kind of week they'd had) they moved onto picking up random tapes and trying to persuade each other that they might be good. Tonight, Becca fancied watching *Mission to Mars* and decided on the following tactic:

'Remember *Mission Impossible*?'

'Of course.'

'And you liked it?'

'It was alright.'

'And you remember it was directed by Brian De Palma.'

'Yeah, what else did he do?' James asked, picking up another tape and reading the summary on the back of the box.

'*Scarface, The Untouchables*.'

'*The Untouchables* was a fucking great film.'

'Do you want to watch something else by him?'

'Costner? OK. What about *The Postman*?'

'I meant De Palma.'

'I know,' he laughed, 'but let's watch *The Postman*.'

Becca looked at her boyfriend, sensing defeat.

'We could do,' she said, 'but I'm not sure you'll like it.'

'Why?'

'It's three hours long.'

'Is it? We don't have to watch all of it if it's shit. Besides, the good Costner movies are always long. *JFK*, what was that cowboy one?'

'*Dances With Wolves*.'

'No, the other one. The one with the bloke out of *Innerspace*.'

'Dennis Quaid. You mean *Wyatt Earp*.'

'Kurt Russell was brilliant in that.'

'Kurt Russell wasn't in *Wyatt Earp*. You're getting it confused with *Tombstone*.'

'But it was the same story, right?'

Becca sighed, and James took the tape to the counter. She wandered over to the shelf of true-life movies, looking for any interesting anomalies. Her favourite to date had been a misplaced copy of *Cocoon*. Followed by a stray *Who Framed Roger Rabbit?*. But they seemed to have hired a more assiduous categorizer since her last visit, and the only film out of place was *The Godfather*.

James unlocked the car and Becca climbed inside, resting the tape on the dashboard.

He looked at her. 'If it's really bad we can turn it off.'

Becca laughed. 'When have you known me to turn a film off? But I know what you're like. You think you want to watch a video and then when we get back you're not interested.'

'That's not true.'

'It is.'

'Only because I want to have sex instead.'

She giggled. 'And you don't think that will happen tonight?'

'I don't think so. But you never know. Three hours is a long time.'

He leaned over and kissed her. Her lips were sore from the cold weather, and after a brief moment she pushed him back.

'Come on, I'm hungry. Let's go get some food.'

Becca's Dodgy Boyfriends #1
Eric

Eric was the first person Becca went out with after finishing university. She had only been living in her aunt's flat for a few months and she was keen to take advantage of finally having a place of her own. Exploring this freedom with Eric, however, was not a good idea.

Eric was an SFX designer for a Spanish film company that specialised in horror-movies. Dedicated to his job, Eric filled Becca's flat with fake bodies and latex monsters. Soon they had so many of these freaky things that she found herself getting attached to them, even coming up with names for some of the more personable creatures.

This aside, the most memorable thing about Eric was that he was a terrible dancer. After one of the film company's sequels was an unexpected success, Eric and his colleagues were flown to a trade event in LA. While out clubbing one night, Eric's dancing was so bad that the other people in the club started imitating him. This prompted a craze called 'the Eric dance', which was later featured in *Details*, *Spin* and *Rolling Stone*.

As with almost all of Becca's previous boyfriends, Eric was the one who finished it. Success went to his head, and he soon started going out with Manda Rose Young, the star of a series of films about a zombie nurse. He took all of his latex with him, except for one small green spaceman called X204 that he let her keep to remember him by.

Chris had spent all afternoon in the kitchen with the stereo up loud, trying to stop himself rushing to the door every time he heard anything that sounded like Diana returning home. It hadn't worked. So far he'd been out to check three times already and was considering going again when the kitchen door opened and she walked in. She was wearing her long cream overcoat and a dark brown dress he hadn't seen before.

'That's nice. Is it new?'

'No, Annabel gave it to me. She thinks it's unlucky.'

'So she gave it to you.'

'Unlucky for her, not me. It's not anything sinister. She just wore it to an audition and didn't get the part.'

'I'm surprised she's got any clothes left.'

Diana laughed. 'Don't be cruel.'

Chris turned round from the oven, and let her hug him. He pressed his face against hers and softly ran his fingers down her back. She patted his arm and walked away.

Almost every time Chris had fallen in love, it had been with someone on the outskirts of whatever social circle he happened to be in. He met Diana at a dinner party. When he arrived, the host had introduced him to a young literary editor, assuming that like many journalists he secretly had a novel or two at the bottom of his sock drawer. They chatted in a desultory fashion, but Chris was much more interested in the dark-haired aspiring actress who'd been introduced as someone who'd done a couple of readings on the host's most recent show.

Every time Chris remembered this evening, he thought of the moment halfway through the meal when Diana had gone from being someone he found attractive to the inevitable next woman in his life. One of the things Chris liked best about movies was that you always knew you were getting the interesting bit; you were seeing someone's whole life summed up in ninety minutes. And when Chris met Diana, he felt his story was about to begin.

He placed Diana's plate in front of her.

'How was Annabel?'

'Good.'

'Jealous about your series?'

'I think so. She was being really nice and magnanimous.'

'Wow. She must be really pissed off.'

Diana laughed. 'She's got a new boyfriend.'

'What's he like?'

'Alright. I don't think they'll stay together long. Annabel kept complaining that he was too nice.'

'Did you tell her about us?'

'Of course.'

'And what did she say?'

'She said it was sad. She thought we made a good couple.'

Chris knew things were over with Diana when he started thinking about how their relationship had failed. The main problem was that Chris couldn't cope with the way Diana handled her depression. And she couldn't change because this was something she'd dealt with all her life. While Diana had grown up in relative luxury, her parents had wanted her to come to terms with her frustration at an early age, and even though she was often unbearably unhappy, they'd always been careful not to trick her out of her misery with treats.

She described her childhood as a series of lost afternoons and her main method of overcoming frustration was to sleep until things were better again. Often she'd even nod off mid-argument, then forget the whole thing when she woke up. If Chris had been a different type of person, this might have proved a useful safety valve for their relationship. Unfortunately, he always lay awake fretting while Diana escaped into sleep.

Chris cleared the plates and Diana went through to the lounge. He came back and sat opposite her, watching as she lifted one long leg over the other.

'Do you want to watch television?' he asked.

'Not really,' she said. 'Why don't you sit next to me?'

'I wasn't sure you'd want me to.'

'Come here.'

He moved and sat next to her, and then immediately got up.

'Actually, I'll just get the wine,' he said.

Looking back down at her, Chris could see how miserable she was just from the way she was holding her body, and hated to think he'd made her like that. When he brought the wine back, he filled the glasses and moved closer to her. She put her arm around him and rubbed his shoulder.

'I missed you,' she said.

'Me too.'

He kissed her neck. She tilted her chin towards him and stroked his hair. He could feel how tense Diana was and longed for her to relax.

'Chris . . .'

'What?' he asked.

'We agreed.'

'One more time, please. It was too sad before.'

'Are you going to be angry afterwards?'

'How could I be angry?'

'I don't know. I'm scared. And confused. I don't want this to end with you shouting at me.'

'I promise that won't happen.'

Chris knew he would remember this last time more than any other, and he wanted it to be perfect. He held Diana until he could sense she was calm and then slowly reached under her dress and started stroking her calves. She lifted her legs over his and lay back against a blue cushion. He didn't want to seem desperate, but at the same time felt scared of being too controlled. And he didn't want Diana to realise that this time was for the benefit of his memory.

He held Diana's hand, and wondered what she was thinking. It occurred to him that she might not have intended to stay this evening. Maybe their lovemaking would be interrupted by the toot of a taxi and he'd have to sit with his trousers round his ankles while she gathered her belongings from upstairs.

After it was over, Chris listened to Diana's chest and wondered whether he should fetch her inhaler. But her breathing slowly returned to normal, and he was so worried about breaking the moment that he didn't want to move. Diana seemed to share this feeling and they both let themselves fall asleep together, messy and naked on the sofa.

Chris's Favourite Films #37
Wings of Desire

Chris first watched *Wings of Desire* with his father when he was sixteen. His mum had been away on a course and his dad had asked if he'd like to see *Throw Momma From the Train*. Chris had agreed to go to the cinema, but said he'd much rather see Wim Wenders' new film. Persuading his father a two-hour black and white film about the afterlife would be more fun than spending ninety minutes in the easygoing company of Danny De Vito and Billy Crystal wasn't easy, but Chris did have a secret weapon. Three months previously Chris had convinced his dad to watch *Paris, Texas* on video and his dad emerged from the experience a changed man. So, once Chris had told him that this new film had a Harry Dean Stanton substitute in the guise of Peter Falk, his dad grudgingly agreed to go.

It wasn't the first time Chris and his dad came out of the cinema with radically different opinions, but it was among the most dramatic. His dad had even sneaked out into the bar during the long middle section, and seemed amazed when Chris emerged talking as if he'd just experienced a religious conversion. It was years later that Chris discovered he wasn't the only one touched by *Wings of Desire*, and although he hadn't seen the film since that day with his dad, it retained a place in his heart.

Becca waited by the door, watching James sleeping. He had crawled to the far left of the bed and was bundling the blue duvet beneath his arm. In his plain white T-shirt, he looked almost as smart in bed as he did during the day. He was far too well groomed for an ad-man, looking more like a model from one of his campaigns. She waited a moment longer, worrying that he might wake up. James slept like he drove, as if it was a job instead of something worth relishing, and was always irritated when Becca got up during the night.

Becca never went near a bed until she'd gathered tissues, water, music, and something to read in case she got bored. In her old flat she'd also taken to bed the phone numbers of friends she'd known would be up late, alone in an edit suite and eager to talk. Sometimes she even took her laptop beneath the sheets, although these days she rarely risked it.

Before she'd moved in with James, insomnia had been so much more enjoyable. None of Becca's previous boyfriends had been especially good sleepers, and most of them had enjoyed staying up late, eating Danish pastries and watching old videos. James had gone to great pains to get her to think of his flat as their shared space, but she'd never really felt comfortable in it. Even with all her stuff (and her belongings easily outnumbered her boyfriend's), she just wasn't as happy here as she'd been in her old flat.

Becca had inherited her flat from her Aunt Nina. She didn't remember much about her, but according to Becca's parents, Becca had been her aunt's favourite. At various times (after school, during university) Becca's parents had suggested she might like to sell the flat. The decision to hold on to it had proved shrewd and the rent money had paid her way all through college. But the flat had proved most useful after she'd finished at Leeds, giving her a base for her post-uni life in London.

She walked to the corner of the lounge that doubled as her workspace, wondering whether or not to log on. The trill before connection might wake James, but she decided to risk it. She had earphones for the stereo and headphones for the TV and video, but using the computer always felt less solitary.

She logged on. No response from James. She found her Discman, slid in a CD, and turned to her keyboard to tap in her name and password. She had mail. Only one, from Jessica. *Everything fine with Chris. Moving in on Sat. Will send paperwork. Jxxxx.* Becca replied to the message, making a joke about *The Lonely Guy*, then logged on to Movielens, her new favourite site.

Movielens was perfect for Becca, and one of the few things on the internet that detained her for more than twenty minutes. Movielens would ask you to rate a hundred and fifty films released in the last three months. Many of the films had yet to come out in England, but this didn't trouble Becca, who felt she had an innate ability to tell whether or not she'd like a film before she'd even seen it.

Once she'd rated the films, she could ask Movielens all kinds of crazy questions. She could ask it to name her favourite musical. Her favourite western released in 1974. Her favourite romantic comedies. And the answers it came up with were always hilarious, no more so than when it told her her favourite films would be *Brazil, The Muppet Movie, Indiana Jones and the Temple of Doom* and *One Flew Over the Cuckoo's Nest.*

After she'd finished playing, Becca pottered out to the

bathroom. She flushed the cistern, washed her hands and opened the door. James stood there, looking bewildered, sleepy and sick.

'Could you make any more fucking noise?'

'I'm sorry,' she said, 'I was trying to be quiet.'

He rubbed his eyes and shook his head. She stepped backwards and he pushed past her, striding towards the toilet. Feeling sorry, Becca turned off all the lights and got back into bed.

They started unpacking slowly and speeded up as six o'clock approached. When it seemed that they weren't going to get the rental van back on time, they emptied what was left onto the pavement and Andy's brother drove it back to the hire shop alone. He returned to find Chris and Andy finishing up the beer.

'Did you make it?' Andy asked.

'Just,' he said, vaulting over the top of the settee and coming down in the space between Chris and Andy.

'So is that it then?' he asked.

'Looks like it.'

'Is the kettle unpacked yet?'

Chris nodded. 'Would you like a coffee?'

'That'd be lovely.'

'Andy?'

He shook his can. 'I'll stick with this.'

Chris walked through to the kitchen. He filled the kettle and put it on, then hovered in the doorway.

'Is that a balcony there?' Andy's brother asked Chris.

'I wouldn't risk standing on it,' said Andy.

'No, but you could put some plants there, couldn't you?'

Chris wandered over to the windows and tried the handle.

'It doesn't open.'

He rattled the handle again.

'Bound to be a key somewhere,' said Andy.

After Andy and his brother had left, Chris brought a box of his papers through to the study and started putting them out on his desk for later. He stacked them in order, the pages he'd written most recently, fruit of his last few late nights, on top. Chris had decided he needed a trip to the supermarket, to get some essentials for the new flat. He would then return and do some work on his book. He looked at his watch. Almost seven. He grabbed his jacket and let himself out, then walked down the shared stairs and onto the street.

Chris was terrible in supermarkets, and rued the day that they started stocking anything other than food. No matter how hungry he was, Chris seemed incapable of a proper shop, much more likely to return with a bag of toy soldiers, some sushi, an ice cream Bounty and a copy of *Heat*.

He found himself wandering towards the sad assortment of videos next to the CD top forty. He couldn't believe he was seriously considering buying a triple-pack of Richard Pryor and Gene Wilder movies. He didn't even like *Stir Crazy* and although he'd yet to see them, doubted *See No Evil, Hear No Evil* or *Another You* would be much good. He remembered the sadness he always felt when he saw single men and women stocking up on comfort films late at night in Tower Records, but it was too late. The box had already reached his basket. He sighed and moved on to the magazines.

It was twenty minutes later when Chris reached the cereal aisle. He saw a woman he fancied picking up a packet of Fibre-1 and tried to remember an article he'd read on the etiquette of supermarket seduction. He knew he was supposed to show he was interested by picking up a box himself, but also that he was supposed to indicate his sexual preference by his choice of cereal. What if he picked a box which meant he was into S&M and she chained him to her bed? Chris had a suspicion that once the woman had noticed him he wouldn't be able to back out, if only because he wouldn't want to disappoint her. So he nervously moved closer to the stacks of boxes and, at the same time as trying to catch her eye, and making sure his hand wasn't rebelling and heading for a packet of Coco Pops, he picked up a box of Sainsbury's own-brand cornflakes. The woman noticed and turned to get a better look at him. Chris tried a thin, hopeful smile, but the woman gave him only the briefest of glances before moving on. Deflated, Chris completed his shop and took his basket to the nearest till.

Walking back, Chris found himself feeling depressed. Shopping alone was much less enjoyable when there was no one waiting for him at home. He tried to think of good things about being single. All he could come up with was being glad that Diana had broken up with him in the autumn. He'd always felt that this was the most romantic season, feeling the sort of stirrings now that most people felt in spring. Almost all of his major romances had started at this time, through school, university and the years afterwards. It was hard to meet people without having a proper job, but he wasn't completely isolated. He could make more of an effort with the students he taught. Or get Andy to introduce him to more people. And besides, it wasn't usually until you were single that you found out who fancied you. He just had to wait and see who came calling.

Chris's Favourite Films #5
Raising Arizona

Chris had only seen his fifth favourite film on video, and knew it would probably go up a place if he ever got to see it in the cinema. The first time he watched it was shortly after it first came out on tape. *Blood Simple* had been on Moviedrome the week before, and he'd wanted to find out more about the Coen brothers. He'd quite liked *Blood Simple,* but he loved *Raising Arizona,* watching it three times before it had to go back to the shop.

Raising Arizona also introduced him to the talents of Nicolas Cage, who for a brief period in the early nineties was to become his favourite actor. Nowadays Cage was less of a hero, but there were a handful of films that convinced Chris the man was a genius (*Wild at Heart, Vampire's Kiss, Zandalee* and *Wings of the Apache*). Watching *Raising Arizona* also made him realise that there was more to John Goodman than his appearances on *Roseanne* suggested, and tipped Chris off about the talents of Holly Hunter.

He didn't think the film was flawless, and the *Mad Max*-style 'baby-hunter' was a bad mistake. But it was probably the funniest comedy he'd ever seen, and as much as he'd enjoyed *Barton Fink, Fargo* and *The Big Lebowski, Raising Arizona* remained his favourite Coen brothers film.

Becca had reached the very last corner of the local video shop, left to decide between two bog-standard erotic thrillers and an action film with Jeff Fahey that held little interest for her. In her hand she held a copy of *The War at Home*, a film way down on her rainy-day list, but likely to be more entertaining than those last three tapes. She flipped the box over to read the back, then, satisfied, she walked up to the counter and gave the old lady her card. As the old lady looked for the tape, Becca tried to work out what she'd been watching on her small television.

It was something with Michael Douglas. *A Perfect Murder*? No, it was *The American President*. Becca couldn't remember too much about the film, or whether she'd enjoyed it. Usually she found the easiest way to trigger her memory was to think about where she'd seen the film and whom she went with. But this time she couldn't recall even those details.

The old lady put the tape on the counter.

'Thanks,' said Becca. 'I don't suppose you remember who directed that film you're watching.'

'The director?' she said slowly. 'I'm sorry, I don't really notice things like that. But it's got that woman who's married to Warren Beatty.'

'Right.'

'I can get the box if you want.'

'No, that's OK. I was just curious. I know I've seen that film but I can't remember anything about it.'

The old lady laughed. 'I'm like that. Sometimes I put on the same tape three or four times without realising it.'

Becca smiled and took the case. Just before she got to the door, she flipped it open and checked it was the right tape inside, then walked out into the street.

As soon as she got home she checked her messages. There were two. The first was from Jessica. The second was a surprise:

'Hi, Becca. This is Scarlett. I know we haven't spoken in a while, and I'm really, really sorry, I've been horrendously busy and haven't had time to do anything, let alone call anyone. Anyway, I don't know if I told you this, but I've been working on this film *Peep Show* and there's a party on Saturday, I mean, it's not a wrap party, but there will be people there from the film . . . it's mostly unknowns but there's a couple of faces you'll recognise. Anyway, it's at my house and you're welcome to bring anyone you want and you only need to ring if you can't make it. OK? Cool.'

Becca stared at the machine, then played the message again. She hadn't been to a party since the end of her last contract. And this would be the real deal, not some boring drinks do with James' business friends. She didn't especially like Scarlett, but had to admit that this was just envy: Scarlett was much more successful than Becca, but also irritatingly and unfailingly generous, always sharing contacts with her friends. Becca hoped that if anything big happened to her she'd behave in the same way, but suspected she'd be too scared about her good fortune running out to share her opportunities with anyone else.

She found a piece of paper and made a note, even though she knew she wouldn't forget. Then she considered calling James right now. But he could be peculiar about social engagements and Becca thought it'd be better to choose her moment. This was a party she couldn't miss.

Next, she picked up the phone and called Jessica.

'Hi, Becca. How are you?'

'Fine. What's happening?'

'Nothing much. I just phoned to tell you Chris called, your new tenant.'

'And?'

'And . . . oh gosh, I know this is going to be really irritating, but do you by any chance have a key for the French windows in your flat?'

Becca went to the deli, bought a sandwich and coffee, and ate it in a nearby park. Then she walked to the nearest tube station and bought a copy of *The Independent* and an all-day travelcard. Although the tube was empty, she walked to the last carriage.

She looked at her watch. Just after one. She reached into her pocket and gripped the keys. Her palms were sweaty and she felt nervous about meeting Chris. She'd told Jessica that David Duchovny wasn't really her type, and it was true, he wasn't, but she found those sort of dark, mysterious looks appealing, and she had a feeling that Chris might turn out to be someone she could fancy.

She'd always enjoyed living in the area where she'd inherited her flat. About half the houses here had been divided into separate flats, while the rest had been sold whole, making the neighbourhood a pleasant mix of young families and stranded singles. While she'd been living here Becca'd loved going for an early evening stroll to the supermarket, finding it fun to look in on people in that twilight time before they pulled their curtains and turned to their TVs.

She stopped outside her old place. Becca was impressed that Chris had already crossed out Rowan's surname and biroed in his own. Somehow from Jessica's description she hadn't imagined he'd be that efficient. She buzzed twice. Waiting for a while seemed a good idea, allowing for the possibility that he was in the bath or maybe even asleep.

Satisfied she wasn't going to be surprised, Becca unlocked the door and walked up the first two flights of stairs, then waited in the hallway for thirty seconds before knocking on Chris's door. She held her breath and gave it another minute, then slid her second key into the lock. Becca knew this wasn't the most sensible course of action, but having come all the way over, she felt like taking a little risk. Holding the key with her fingers wrapped round the metal to minimise the click, she turned it clockwise and opened the door.

'Hello?' she called.

No response. Well, now she was inside, there was no point leaving the keys without a note. He'd understand if she went to his desk and found a piece of paper, wouldn't he? Of course he would. She breathed out and locked the door behind her, so that if he did return unexpectedly she'd have a chance to hide.

Becca'd never really figured out why she felt so comfortable in this space. Of course, it helped that she'd known these rooms since she was born, but there was more to it than that. She'd never felt this way about the family home, and similarly, wasn't the sort of woman who usually got sentimental about where she lived. Even sneaking in here now she felt the flat welcoming her, and was about to go out to the kitchen to make herself a coffee before she remembered this probably wasn't a good idea.

She stood in the doorway. OK, she told herself, leave the key and let's go. But she couldn't shake an irresistible urge to have a quick scout around. She told herself that she wouldn't open any drawers, or snoop, or go looking for any secrets, but there wasn't any harm in just looking, was there?

She could tell it was a man living here. Becca was messy herself, but there was a difference between a man's mess and a woman's mess. Women's mess was intentional, a scattering of clues that didn't reveal anything they didn't want known. A man's mess, however, was much more disheartening, a territorial warning instead of a psychological invitation. Still, she had to remember that he hadn't been expecting a visitor and that if this was Chris unzipped – so to speak – the place wasn't really all that bad.

She could've done without the bundled clothes by the sofa and the crusty takeaway carton on top of the coffee table, but it wasn't as if she'd never left that sort of stuff out herself. The rest of the mess looked much more interesting, especially the black and white photographs scattered around the desk.

Becca walked across the room and leaned down for a closer look. Film stills, taken from a wide range of movies, but mainly *Speed 2, Stolen Hearts, Forces of Nature, The Net* and *While You Were Sleeping*. Oh God, she thought, not a Sandra Bullock obsessive. Becca knew she'd never be able to be friends with anyone whose favourite actress was Sandra Bullock. Or Julia Roberts. Meg Ryan she could cope with, but those other two, no way.

She looked up and noticed her *Drugstore Cowboy* poster through his bedroom doorway. Time for a flip through her tenant's video collection. Becca was surprised Chris hadn't put up any posters himself, especially after what Jessica had said about how taken he'd been with the one she'd left hanging. But some boys were like that, not wanting to be too showy about their tastes.

This theory was borne out by the fact that all his videos were hidden inside a large wooden cabinet. She opened the cabinet and was immediately surprised by what she found inside. *Clueless, Romy and Michelle's High School Reunion, The Wedding Singer, When Harry Met Sally, Sleepless in Seattle, Michael, Shampoo, The Graduate, Kramer vs Kramer* . . . the guy was clearly either a romantic or a retard. Even with the Sandra Bullock photos she hadn't been expecting this.

Where was the guy stuff? *The Godfather, Pulp Fiction, Once Upon a Time in the West.* She skimmed down the rest of the stack and was relieved to see that after the top twenty titles, things started to get a bit more normal. A few David Lynch films, *Europa,* some Scorsese. Still, this was a pretty weird collection. She found a copy of *Evita* and wondered if he might be gay.

OK, she told herself, I'm only supposed to be getting a piece of paper. She sat down at the desk in his study, looked through the scraps of paper and cinema tickets, and then turned over the pages on his desk until she found a blank pad and a fountain pen. She wrote a note, and took it back out to the table by the door. Leaving the keys and message, she unlocked the door and walked out.

'Surely you don't agree that *Basic Instinct* is as good a film as *Vertigo*?'

Chris looked at his watch, aware that they had entered the free-fall part of his lesson. He knew that most of his students liked this bit best, and that they only sat through the screenings and listened to his potted histories so they could have these little arguments just before he sent them all home.

His class split into roughly three groups. There were the mad old men, who tended to say least in this last section; the Sunday-supplement readers (who seemed to know everything about the week's big movies without ever having seen them, parroting the opinions of Philip French or Gilbert Adair); and the genuine movie-nuts.

Chris liked the movie-nuts best. Unlike the Sunday-supplement crowd, who were mainly in their early thirties, the nuts numbered a variety of different ages and backgrounds. There were the Taranteenies (still a living breed years after *Pulp Fiction*), but there was also a recently divorced woman who seemed to spend every night in the cinema, and a quiet Asian man who was either a compulsive liar or had genuinely seen every film ever made, including many Chris was convinced he'd made up.

'Well,' said Chris, 'part of the point of tonight's talk was supposed to be that classic films aren't *necessarily* more entertaining than modern movies, even when the modern movies are remakes and rip-offs. Take, for example, the two versions of *Cat People*.'

The old men started sitting up. Chris had shown the Paul Schrader version the previous week and they'd all got rather overexcited about Nastassja Kinski.

'Or the two *Scarface*s. Very different films, and it may not be instructive to compare them.'

'But what about when the remake is obviously shit. Like *Diabolique*,' chipped in one of the class.

'Ah,' said Chris, 'but is the remake obviously shit?'

'Yes,' cried an exasperated voice from the back.

'I don't know. There's a curious *flatness* to that film which is really unique.'

'But that's just you being weird. It's not what the filmmaker intended.'

'Like I keep telling you, what the filmmaker intended is of no consequence. Movies belong to us, and we're free to watch them in any way we see fit.'

The class started laughing.

'What?' Chris asked.

'You sound like Robin Williams,' said Deborah, one of the Sunday-supplement types. 'Any minute now you're going to get us up on our desks chanting the names of shit movies.'

They laughed again, and Chris looked down at the pen in his hand. He was glad it was coming to the end of the lesson because he sensed his students were just about to reach the point of mutiny. It didn't seem right that he was teaching, especially as he had no real interest in sharing his opinions. And his qualifications for being in front of a blackboard were ridiculously slight. If anyone properly challenged his authority he'd concede in a second, and sensed that not only did the class know this, but also that the only reason they didn't disrupt proceedings was because they enjoyed his charade.

Chris had never wanted to teach. He only took the class because it gave a semblance of structure to his week, and because being a teacher (even only of night-classes once or twice a week) seemed to legitimise a person in the eyes of the world. That and the fact that the meagre amount it brought in coupled with the odd bit of reviewing just about kept the wolf from the door. Even though every teacher Chris had ever met had depressed him in some way, people still seemed to believe it was an honourable profession, and Chris enjoyed not having to explain himself further.

'OK,' said Chris, 'I guess that's it. Next week's lesson starts at six-thirty instead of seven, and we'll be watching *The Passenger.*'

He waited by the blackboard, wondering who'd ask him to the pub tonight. He usually made his decision depending on who asked. Tonight, however, he'd already decided to go straight home after the lesson, and turned down the offer even though the class sent forward Nadine, his favourite student.

He picked up his jacket, shrugged it on and walked to the bus stop. The Lomax Centre was twenty minutes from his new flat, and he was glad it wasn't raining as he waited for the bus, wondering whether there was anything he could salvage from tonight's lesson for his book.

Chris's Favourite Films #52
Teen Wolf

Everyone at Chris's school liked *Back to the Future* – even his English teacher, Mr Douglas, who only saw one film a year and invariably hated the experience – but Chris and his friends admired the film without really enjoying it. It seemed too self-consciously a 'family entertainment', being fun but having no real bite.

Then, a couple of weeks later, *Teen Wolf* hit the cinema. Suddenly Chris understood the boyish appeal of Michael J. Fox. He seemed so much more endearing as a werewolf than a time-traveller, and the film had an illicit teenage quality that *Back to the Future* lacked. It felt bad for you, like staying up late to watch *Married . . . With Children*. It was that quality that led to Chris and his friends rediscovering the film years later, trying out the car-surfing and doing the Teen Wolf dance at night-clubs. It was so perfectly eighties, the kind of film they didn't make any more.

Chris knew it was no classic, but he was surprised at how well it held up, and although he hadn't watched it all the way through in years, he occasionally put it on for five minutes or so when he needed cheering up.

Becca had been really careful about picking the right moment to bring up Scarlett's party. She'd taken on board everything James had said about how stressful he found it when she confronted him with all her news the moment he got through the door, and how when she really wanted something she automatically assumed he wouldn't want her to have it. So she waited till he had time to wind down, floated the suggestion as if his response didn't matter, and was amazed to discover that he was totally up for it.

They were both quite excited on Saturday afternoon, unable to really concentrate on anything (including the *Brookside* omnibus), and set off earlier than they'd intended, taking a taxi over to Scarlett's place just after seven. She hadn't specified a time, and Becca had been worried they'd turn up to find no one there, but the party was already so packed that even the hallway was lined with people. Becca saw Scarlett on the stairs and made eye contact with her. Scarlett came across and took them both by the hand.

'Hi, kids. I wasn't sure if you'd show up.'

'We were worried we'd set off too early.'

'Oh no, the party's been going since three o'clock. There was some sort of shooting fuck-up so we just came back here and started the celebrations early. What would you like to drink?'

'What've you got?' James asked.

Scarlett looked at the paper-wrapped wine bottle they'd brought with them.

'Oh well, I meant to say this on the phone but I guess I

forgot. It's supposed to be a vodka party. But don't worry, I'll take your wine and hide it for when the vodka's run out and everybody's desperate. That's unless you don't like vodka. I mean, I know you like vodka, Becca, but what about you, James?'

'Vodka's fine.'

'Great. Come with me to the kitchen.'

She pulled them behind her through the lounge. Although it was still early, the dimmed lighting made it seem much later, as did the advanced inebriation of her guests. Becca felt disappointed that everyone was already so drunk, especially as she'd seen tonight as an opportunity for some decent and much-needed networking. James, however, seemed excited by the state everyone was in, as if pleased to be surrounded by such decadence.

They reached the kitchen. Scarlett leaned down to open the fridge. Becca noticed her boyfriend looking down their host's top, but chose to ignore it, not wanting to spoil the evening with unnecessary jealousy. A girl in a striped top sat behind them, talking to a man with Jesus Christ hair and a stubby goatee.

'So what do you want with your drinks? Tonic? Cranberry?'

'Cranberry would be lovely.'

'OK. James?'

'Um, tonic, please.'

'Right.' She pulled out a bottle of Absolut. 'Sorry it's not Stoli, but we ran out of that early. Now can you see any glasses?'

Becca and James exchanged looks. Scarlett turned to them for a moment, then placed the bottle on the kitchen top and ran out into the lounge. The girl in the striped top jumped down and slipped out of the kitchen. The Jesus guy offered his hand to James.

'Hi, I'm Joel.'

'Hi, Joel. I'm James and this is Becca.'

Joel nodded and put his hand to his neck. He was wearing a black T-shirt with pink neon lettering across his chest. He looked distracted.

'You don't have any gear, do you?'

'No, sorry.'

'That's OK, I don't really want it. It's just if you had any . . .'

'We don't.'

He looked away. 'How do you know Scarlett?'

'I don't really. She's Becca's friend.'

He nodded.

'How about you?'

Joel sat back and took a long look at James. 'Through the film. I'm the screenwriter.'

'Oh, right, sorry. What's the project called?'

Joel pointed at the lettering on his T-shirt.

'That's what it's called?' asked James. *'Peep Show?'*

'That's the working title. We're a bit worried people might get it muddled up with *Peeping Tom.'*

'What's that?'

'Michael Powell, 1960,' Becca interrupted, smiling at Joel.

Joel looked impressed, but said in a bored tone, 'That was an easy one.'

'OK. Try me again.'

'Powell and Pressburger or something else?'

'Anything.'

'OK. The Rocky films, in order.'

Scarlett appeared in the doorway. 'Sorry I took a while. That's the problem with hosting these occasions. You have to be nice to everyone. Anyway, I've got the glasses.'

She turned away and poured their drinks.

'What about you, Joel? Are you alright for the moment?'

'I'll have a refill, if one's going.'

'OK, give me your glass.'

Scarlett poured him his drink, then took James' arm and steered him into the other room. Becca felt a bit anxious about letting her boyfriend go off with Scarlett, and didn't want to get stuck with this earnest film-boy, but realised that if either of them were going to enjoy the party, it was probably best they separated. She watched James and Scarlett meld into another group and looked back at Joel.

'So are you in the business, Becca?'

'Sort of,' she said. 'More TV than film.'

'Any credits I might recognise?'

'Well, the last thing I worked on was a travel programme called *Run at the Sun*.'

Joel nodded. 'I saw that.'

Becca looked at him, amazed. 'Did you?'

'In the schedules, I mean. I didn't actually watch it.'

'Right.'

He leaned back against the fridge. 'So come on, give me a date for the first Rocky.'

'I don't know. Do you have the dates committed to memory?'

'Well, no, but I bet Scarlett has a film guide somewhere.'

Becca followed Joel over to where Scarlett was standing with James in a group that included two men in suits and a notably attractive woman with pale skin and black hair. It seemed weird that men would wear suits to a weekend party like this, but then there were always peculiar people involved in any film production and they were probably just financial contributors who Scarlett wanted to show a good time.

Scarlett seemed surprised that they'd come across and kept looking at Joel while one of the suited men talked to James and the dark-haired woman. When the man finally paused, Joel leaned in.

'Sorry to interrupt. Scarlett, do you have a film guide here?'

The first suited man laughed. 'Here you go, Scarlett. Time to prove yourself.'

'Of course,' said Scarlett, 'but it's in my study.'

'That's OK. We can go up.'

'It's locked,' she said, and lifted a thin purple ribbon from around her neck and over her head. Attached to the ribbon was a small metal key.

'Right,' said Joel. 'Which room is it?'

'Ah,' said Scarlett, 'that's not the study key.'

'OK.' Joel put his fist on his hip. 'Tell me the riddle.'

'No riddle. That's the key to the cupboard under the stairs. In the cupboard are two keys. The one with the blue blob of nail varnish is the key to my bedroom. The one with the pink varnish is the key to my study. That's the one you want.'

James laughed. 'Do you have this sort of organisation on your set?'

Scarlett looked at him. 'It'll all go to pot in a couple of hours. I'm just a bit paranoid because last time I had a party someone shat in my bed.'

Becca looked at her friend, surprised she'd say something so weird in front of her guests. She knew James would find the comment distasteful, and was gratified to see him move slightly from Scarlett, getting closer to the dark-haired woman. Becca thought the woman looked familiar and wondered whether they'd worked together.

'Come on then, Becca, let's finish our mission.'

Joel took her hand and dragged her out of the lounge. The contact surprised Becca and she hoped Joel hadn't started fancying her. There were lots of people in the hallway, most of whom seemed disgruntled when Joel started shunting them aside.

'Did she say pink or blue?'

'Pink, I think. Maybe blue.'

'Let's take both.'

He grinned at her and closed the cupboard door. Scarlett had appeared beside them and touched Becca lightly on the arm.

'Make sure it's locked afterwards, OK?'

Joel led the way upstairs. He was wearing oversized trainers and the people staking out the stairs had to shuffle aside to let him through.

'Which door do you think it is?'

'Try the one at the end.'

Joel pushed his hand down on the top banister and jumped down the landing. Looking round and smiling at her, he kneeled to unlock the door. It opened first time. Becca followed down behind him, eager to get a look at whatever Joel thought was so impressive. Joel went inside while Becca stayed by the doorway, looking round. The G4 on Scarlett's desk was the first thing she noticed, but she felt even more envious of the three walls of videos and reference books. Joel walked across and kneeled down beside Scarlett's desk.

'*Halliwell's, Maltin's, Video Hound, The Bare Facts Movie Guide.*' Joel stopped to pull out this volume. 'I thought it was only sad old men who had a copy of this.'

'I've looked at it,' she said distractedly. 'It'd be fun if it wasn't for all those references to buns.'

He slid the book back in. 'Surely that's the whole point.'

'I know, it's the word I don't like. It sounds, I don't know, too American porn.'

He pulled out the *Time Out Film Guide*. 'OK, *Rocky I.*'

'Seventy-nine,' she replied.

'For which one?'

'The first one.'

'No, seventy-nine is *Rocky II*. But I'll give you a point anyway. Now, do you want to have another try for the first one?'

'Seventy-six.'

'Congratulations. Two out of two. Now, part three?'

By now, Becca had remembered that most sequels in the seventies and eighties tended to come at three-year intervals, and guessed right again:

'Eighty-two.'

'Fantastic. And four?'

'Eighty-five.'

'Wow,' said Joel, 'and you pretended you didn't know. Part five?'

Becca paused. Embarrassed that she'd actually started to take this challenge seriously, she nevertheless felt an urge to get this last one right. She knew there was a longer gap between the last sequel and the first four films, but couldn't quite remember how long it was.

'And I can be a year out either way?'

'Yep.'

'OK, eighty-nine.'

'Close enough, ninety. Congratulations.' He handed her the book. 'Now you do me.'

'What?'

'Pick a film with some sequels and we'll see if I'm as good as you.'

'Don't you want to get back to the party?'

'In a minute. Come on, you can't deny me my fun.'

Becca exhaled, and looked down at her feet. She was worried that James might be getting the wrong idea about her disappearing upstairs with Joel, and didn't want him getting upset. Still, Joel seemed pretty insistent. She looked for a film with only one or two sequels.

'OK,' she said, '*Porky's*.'

'Good choice,' Joel grinned. 'Now let's see . . . I think part one came out in . . . eighty, two in eighty three and three in eighty five.'

'Correct.'

He reached out for her arm. 'All of them? Completely right?'

'Well, within a year or so.'

He smiled. 'Do I get a prize?'

'You get half a prize.'

'Do I choose what I get?'

She looked at him. 'That depends. What did you have in mind?'

'A kiss.'

'Can you have half a kiss?'

'I don't know. Maybe you could just use your top lip.'

'No, Joel, I don't think that's a good idea.'

He blinked.

'Shall we go back downstairs?' she asked gently.

'OK.'

She returned the guide to the shelf and followed Joel out of the room. She waited while he locked the door, then went down with him to put the keys back in the cupboard. Then the two of them walked back to join Scarlett, James, the dark-haired woman and the two suited men.

'Did you lock it?' Scarlett asked.

'Of course,' said Joel, 'and we put the keys back in the downstairs cupboard.'

'Great. Who'd like another vodka?'

James nodded, and handed Scarlett his glass. Joel and Becca did the same.

'Everyone else OK?' She looked round. 'Good. James, I'll leave you to do the introductions.'

Scarlett walked back towards the kitchen. Becca looked at her boyfriend, waiting to see how he'd handle his appointed task.

'Um, OK, Becca and . . .'

'Joel.'

'Joel, this is Keith, Derek and Diana.'

Smiles and handshakes exchanged, Becca focused on Diana.

'Are you working on the movie?'

Diana tilted her head down, lips forming a small smile. 'Not this time.'

'But you are in the business?'

'Well,' she said, 'I'm an actress.'

'Oh, right, I thought you looked familiar, but assumed it was because we'd worked together.'

'What do you do?'

'I work for a channel you've never heard of. The last show I worked on was called *Run at the Sun.*'

'Right. Well, I'm still really at the very beginning of my screen career. I've been doing theatre before now, and adverts. Although I'm about to start a series for Channel Five.'

'What's it called?'

'*Kiss.*'

'Catchy title.'

'D'you think so? I was worried it was a bit corny.'

'No, it's good. I'd notice it in the listings.'

'What's the show about?' Joel asked.

'Well, it's quite ambitious, although I think the concept will end up being better than the execution.' She looked down at the carpet, then launched into her explanation. 'The idea is that it starts off as a serial and turns into a soap opera, although unlike normal soap operas where it's like lots of simultaneous, intertwining story lines, this is more like one story that's followed to the end, and then another story that's connected to the first one, and gradually you build up a mental picture of all the different people and how they're all involved in each other's lives.'

'Sounds complicated,' said James.

'It is, but the good thing about it is that even if I'm not in the next story, I'll almost definitely end up coming back into it later.'

'What's your story about?'

'My story?' She swallowed. 'I really should've worked out my spiel by now. Basically, the overarching plot for the whole thing is that there are these eight women who were at university together. The main character is called Heather and I play a friend of hers called Pamela. The first part of the series starts with me not in contact with any of the women apart from a girl called Amber who lives with me. Amber's bisexual, and she's got a crush on me.' She paused, as Scarlett reappeared with the drinks. 'Is this too much detail?'

'That depends,' said Scarlett. 'Who's it about?'

'It's not gossip,' Diana said quickly.

'It's the plot of Diana's new series,' James explained, 'the opening story.'

Becca looked at her boyfriend, realising he was impressed with this pale-skinned, dark-haired woman, with her TV series and her made-up love life. Becca knew Scarlett wouldn't be pleased that the men's attention was elsewhere and smirked as she said,

'Oh, I'm sorry, and do carry on. It all sounds fascinating.'

Becca could tell Diana had been put out by the interruption, and probably expected more coaxing before resuming her story, but also that she was too eager to sulk for long.

'OK,' said Diana, 'Amber's got a crush on me, and she's trying to persuade me to get closer to her. Ultimately, she'd probably like me to fall in love with her, but in the meantime she just wants to be my friend. But we've got quite a complicated relationship because the main reason why I'm not in contact with the other women I used to live with is because I had this massive falling-out with Heather and she's cast me out of the group. Amber's always felt a little bit of an outsider anyway because of her sexuality, and Heather's always held her at arm's length because she knows that Amber's had much more experience and is basically a much wilder person.'

'Sounds a bit dodgy,' Scarlett muttered.

'What?'

'Well, you know, the bisexual being cast as a promiscuous character.'

'I didn't say she was promiscuous.'

'Sorry, more experienced.'

Diana looked serious. 'That's a good point. But the thing about Amber is that the actress who plays her is so talented and attractive that it's not really important whether she's a good or bad person.'

'Right,' said Scarlett, 'go on with the story.'

'OK. My character is incredibly insecure, especially when it comes to men. The whole reason I fell out with Heather was to do with a man, or two men, I don't know yet because that story's being held back for much later in the series.'

'This all sounds very compelling,' said Keith. 'I had no idea there were shows of that depth. Whenever I watch soaps they always seem so two-dimensional.'

'We've got a very good writer,' Diana smiled. 'Have you heard enough or shall I go on? I don't feel I've done a very good job of explaining my plot.'

'No, no,' Keith nodded, 'do carry on.'

'OK, and I'll get to the point now, I promise. Basically, what happens is that Amber is probably as insecure as I am, but she disguises it by befriending needy people and then making them think she's massively confident. So when the first episode starts I'm totally in awe of her, and she's kind of in love with me. Or maybe pretending to love me, but the point is that I feel loved. And this allows me to take control of the situation by holding her at a distance, mainly because I'm straight, but also because I'm scared of being in love. This is OK for a while and then this guy comes along who's, like, totally in love with me. And although I'm scared because of this undisclosed thing in my past, I start to let him into my life. Of course, Amber is really jealous, and tries to make things difficult for us.

'And because I have all these weird self-esteem issues, I decide that Amber would make a much better partner for him than me and push them together, hoping that nothing's going to happen, but of course they fall in love and the whole thing drives me slightly crazy and I try to kill myself and end up in hospital and that's how the next story begins, with Heather and the other girls forgiving me and coming to visit me and then the series goes off to follow their lives.'

Diana smiled as she finished her story, looking round for approval. The suited guys, Keith and Derek, seemed most impressed, but Becca could tell James was also entranced. There was a pause while everyone digested what Diana had told them.

'That really does sound great,' said Becca. 'And when will it be on television?'

'I don't know exactly yet. Probably next summer.'

'Cool.' She looked at Keith and Derek. 'Sorry, I think I missed quite an important part of the earlier conversation. What is it you guys do again?'

Becca was surprised how sober she felt when they took a taxi home around two. The vodkas had kept coming, but had had little effect, even though she'd never been a big drinker and hadn't got wasted in a while so her tolerance was down. James, however, was really drunk, and had even downed a pint glass of the wine they'd brought with them just before Scarlett called the taxi.

'That was fun, wasn't it?' he said as they clambered into the back of the cab.

'Yeah, thanks for coming with me.'

'No, no, you know you never have to persuade me when it comes to something like that. I love your glamorous film-star parties.'

'And how did you like the glamorous film star?'

'Who?'

'Diana.'

'She wasn't a film star. She was doing TV.'

'Still, what did you think of her?'

James blinked. 'I thought she was very friendly. And her TV show sounded very interesting.'

'Yes, I suppose so.'

'Didn't you think so?'

'Well, she went on about it a bit, didn't she?'

'A little bit, but she did have a complicated plot to explain. And it's not like you don't get excited when you're working on a new project.'

Becca didn't reply.

'Well, you do, don't you? It's human nature. That's what it's like when you love your job. If I was starring in a TV series, you wouldn't be able to stop me talking about it.'

'I don't think she was exactly starring in the series.'

James laughed.

'What?' Becca demanded.

'Nothing.'

'Oh, fuck off.'

'Come on, Becca,' he said, putting his arm around her back and trying to pull her towards him, 'don't be angry. It was a really nice night.'

Becca let James hold her, knowing she was being unfair. It was only natural that Diana would impress him, and she should've known that she'd come away from Scarlett's party feeling inadequate. Becca wished she was drunk enough to get away with a stupid argument. But she already felt annoyed about how much she'd given away, and decided she'd feel better if she just closed her eyes and stopped talking.

Chris opened his desk drawer and took out his alarm clock. He always kept it there while he wrote, finding it too much of a distraction to have the time constantly in sight. Beneath the Tristar logo, the time read one a.m. He couldn't believe he'd let it get so late.

Writing at night was something he hadn't done since university, and he was surprised how addictive the habit had become. Tonight he'd sat down at ten to see if he could work up a few ideas before heading to Scarlett's party and ended up writing continuously for almost three hours.

He put the clock back in the drawer and wondered whether it was worth getting a taxi over to Scarlett's. The party would probably be dying down, but there might still be a few people he knew, and more importantly, Diana would've almost definitely have left.

There were blinds instead of curtains in the flat and Chris kept them up while he worked. Not because he wanted to spy on his neighbours, but because he enjoyed the idea that the people living in the flats opposite might notice him as he worked. He remembered reading something in a magazine a few years before about an elderly science-fiction author who wrote in shop windows, pinning pages to the glass as he completed them. While Chris doubted he could cope with that level of attention, he enjoyed his mini-version of this technique, thinking it a good way of combating the solitude of writing. It was also reassuring to know he wasn't the only person up this late.

Chris stood up and leaned in closer to the window, inspecting the flats opposite. There didn't seem to be anyone awake on the second floor, but he could see two lights on the third. One of the lights appeared to come from a desk lamp, and Chris watched the pale face of the woman also still up, feeling a sexy kinship with this unknown stranger and wondering what she was working on.

Chris realised he'd been at the window too long and that the woman opposite had stopped writing and was now staring at him. He wanted to make some gesture that'd convince her he wasn't spying, but realised whatever he did now would be construed as suspicious. So he turned away and walked out to his kitchen, enjoying a fantasy about walking over to the woman's flat, ringing her doorbell and being welcomed in by her.

He went to the fridge, poured himself a glass of orange juice, and thought about the party. Andy would probably still be there, after all, as he was always the last to leave any gathering, and it'd be fun to surprise him with a late appearance.

Chris picked up the phone. He knew he should just bite the bullet and call another taxi service, but couldn't bring himself to do it. Andy's brother had told him, several times, that if he ever found out Chris had been in any cab other than his, he'd never speak to him again. There had been occasions when Chris had ignored Andy's brother's commandment, but only in unavoidable circumstances.

'Hi, Chris,' he said, 'I've been waiting for your call.'

'Really?' Chris asked, slightly spooked.

'You're going to the same party as Andy, right?'

'Has he not gone yet?'

'Yeah, I dropped him off earlier. But he said you'd phone.'

Chris made a mental note to kill Andy.

'Where are you now?'

'On my way over. I'll see you in fifteen minutes.'

He was as good as his word. Showing surprising consideration for the late hour, Andy's brother walked up to Chris's door
instead of sounding his horn from the street in the time-
honoured tradition. Chris followed him to the taxi.

He sat in the back.

'Good night?' he asked, even though he knew Andy's
brother rarely had any conventional business.

'Not bad.'

'Do you want me to pass out your card at the party?'

'Andy's already doing that. But thanks.'

A Tom Waits song came on the stereo. Chris couldn't tell
which one, but he recognised the voice. It seemed appropriate
for the hour, and made him think of *Night on Earth*. He realised
he hadn't brought anything to drink.

'You don't know any late-night off-licences, do you?' he
asked Andy's brother.

'What are you after?'

'I don't know.' Chris thought for a moment, wondering
what would be most appreciated at this time of night. 'Spirits.
A bottle of whisky or vodka.'

'There aren't many places round here. I do know somewhere
that'll serve you. It's a bit out of the way, though.'

'That's fine.'

He nodded, and turned the wheel. After three Tom Waits
songs had croaked to conclusion, he said,

'Chris, if I tell you something, do you promise not to tell my
brother?'

'OK.'

Chris could see Andy's brother trying to get a better look at
him in the rear-view mirror. He was by far the most relaxed
member of his family, although tonight he looked a little
agitated.

'It's no big secret. I just don't want Andy to know because he'll make fun of me.'

'OK. What is it?'

'I've been working on a screenplay.'

Chris laughed. 'But I thought you hated films.'

'No,' he said, sincerely, 'I just hate listening to Andy going on about them all the time.'

Chris didn't know how to answer this, wondering if Andy's brother felt the same way about him. After a moment, he asked,

'What's it about?'

'My screenplay?'

'Yeah.'

He stopped the car. 'Go get your drink first. I'll tell you when you come back.'

'Where am I going?'

'The kebab shop. If you want vodka, ask for the Special. If you want whisky . . . actually, I think that's the Special as well. Never mind, he'll probably give you the choice. Just ask for the Special, OK?'

'OK.'

Chris got out of the taxi and walked up to the shop. There were three people already waiting in front of him. He realised they'd already had their orders taken, and caught the eye of the man serving.

'Can I have the Special, please?'

The man held his gaze. 'What flavour sauce?'

'Vodka.'

The man laughed and surreptitiously brought up a bottle from beneath the counter. He wrapped it in chip paper and handed it to Chris.

'That'll be fifteen pounds, please,' the man said.

*

'Did you get what you wanted?' Andy's brother asked.

Chris nodded. 'Tell me about your screenplay.'

He looked over his shoulder. 'It's a cross between *Look Who's Talking* and *Apocalypse Now*. I haven't seen either of 'em but I know what they're about. But anyway, my film's about a baby who accidentally gets drafted into the army and has to go to Vietnam.'

'A comedy then?'

He nodded. 'I've thought out all the main set pieces. There could be a bit when there's a hard-nut colonel character handing out rifles down a row of soldiers and he gives one to the baby and the baby falls in the mud. And a bit at the end where all the helicopters come down and you see the baby leading the attack.'

Chris didn't know what to say. Andy's brother continued driving in silence.

'Can you picture it?' he asked.

'Yeah, why not? You'd probably want to make the whole world consistently crazy though. Like in *Being John Malkovich*.'

He shook his head. 'I haven't seen that film, but I don't want it to be surreal at all. I want the whole thing to be done entirely realistically. It'll be much funnier if the audience identifies with the baby.'

Chris murmured agreement. Andy's brother seemed satisfied with his response and allowed him to sit back until they reached Scarlett's house.

'Have a good night,' he told him, 'and call me later if you need a lift home.'

'OK.' Chris got out of the car and gave Andy's brother a fiver. He walked up the front path to Scarlett's surprisingly suburban redbrick house. Now he'd reached the party he was glad he'd made the effort, especially when the door opened and he could see the party was still in full flow. He looked for Scarlett and

Andy, but couldn't see them. A few people were dancing to Madonna in the lounge. Almost every time Chris went to a party the inevitable argument about which CD to put on ended when someone brought out *The Immaculate Collection*. And once it went on, it took a brave man to try to replace it.

He walked through the lounge, and checked the staircase. Although there were lots of people spread up the stairs, there was no one he recognised. He went through to the kitchen.

'Darling,' said Scarlett, kissing him, 'I thought you weren't coming.'

'Sorry I'm late. Is Andy still here?'

She took his bottle of vodka. 'No, he left with the sound engineer.'

Chris laughed. 'Pretty?'

'Not bad. Although I must admit I was surprised when I saw them talking. She's quite acerbic. And unlikely to be impressed with all his film reviewer talk.'

'He'll probably show her his pictures of him arm-wrestling Tim Roth. That usually does the trick.'

She looked at him, giving him a smile that made him feel clever and naughty. He loved being friends with Scarlett. He watched her kneel down and bring up a bottle of tonic from the fridge. 'Thanks for bringing the vodka. We were running out.'

'No problem. So are you pleased with the film?'

'Oh, it's not finished yet.' She looked up. 'But it's going well.'

'Good.'

She handed him a glass. 'So tell me about you and Diana.'

'How much do you know?'

'Only what I heard from Andy. Have you really split up?'

'Yeah.'

'For ever and ever? No hope of reconciliation?'

'I doubt it.'

'What happened?'

'She got a part in a new TV show.'

'So I hear.'

Chris looked at her. 'She told you about it?'

'She told everyone about it.'

He smiled. 'She's so pleased. And it is great. She's waited so long for this sort of break.'

'So what was the problem?'

'I got jealous. I was used to having her to myself. And to her being out of work. Even when she was really dangerously depressed, it made me feel good that I was looking after her. Sometimes I felt like I was the only person in the world who she trusted.'

'Because you believed in her?'

'Exactly. But now everyone else believes in her.' He swallowed a mouthful of vodka. 'I knew it was only a matter of time.'

She stood up, pressing her back against the fridge. 'So why did you break up? Because you were being possessive?'

'Something like that. Maybe she thought she had to be single to be successful.'

Scarlett considered this. 'What are you doing on Monday?'

'Not much. Why?'

'Come to a screening with me. My friend Bob has a new film. I'm not sure if it'll be any good, but it should be a laugh.'

'OK,' said Chris, 'I'd like that.'

'You promise you'll come?'

He nodded. 'It's a date.'

Becca turned over, checked the clock and fell back against the mattress. Eleven-twenty. This was the third day running she hadn't noticed James leave. It wasn't so bad when she woke up to him showering and couldn't be bothered to get out of bed. But for her boyfriend to be able to wake up, wash, eat breakfast and leave the house all without her realising was ridiculous. What made it worse was that she suspected he was deliberately doing everything quietly, pretending he was concerned about waking her but really getting a sanctimonious pleasure from observing her sloth.

She pulled the duvet around her body, then took the remote from the bedside table and switched on the television. At the beginning of her time at home she'd protected herself from daytime TV by only watching videos, knowing that the former was a much more dangerous addiction. Now she spent as much time watching chat shows and soaps as she did with Mickey Rourke.

Becca got out of bed and went downstairs to pick up the post. A telephone bill. She left it on the mat, went back up, checked her ansaphone, then logged on. Since seeing Scarlett's set-up the previous Saturday she'd been unable to get any pleasure out of her small workspace. It suddenly seemed obvious that this was the reason why her career was progressing so slowly. No wonder Scarlett was successful. Every time she went into her office she probably felt like Steven Spielberg.

She had three e-mails. One from her mother, another from James reminding her to video a programme he wanted to watch, and a junk-mail from a site she'd visited once by accident inviting her to buy stereo equipment. Depressed, she switched off the computer and went back into the bedroom.

Becca got back under the duvet. She'd been feeling down since the party, unsure whether she was more upset about being out of work or because things were getting stale between her and James. She didn't want to break up with him, or go out with anyone else, but she felt a desperate need for some sort of excitement. She'd been toying with the idea of going back to Chris's flat all week, trying to provoke James into arguments so that he'd give her a reason for further developing her secret life. But he'd refused to oblige. Eventually, she'd convinced herself that her tiny act of invasion came from a grander dissatisfaction with the state of her existence. Surely that was a motivation any Hollywood actress would be able to grasp.

Sloppy dressing, like daytime TV, was another home-alone habit that Becca had only managed to resist for the first few days of her stretch. She'd long since stopped worrying that James might go off her if he saw her wearing the same clothes three days running, and had never been concerned about the old Italian man in the deli. Today, however, she wanted to change into something clean, and took a red top and a pair of laundered jeans from her cupboard.

Becca locked the door behind her, just as she'd done on her previous visit. She felt even more excited than she had on her first trip here, and told herself that despite her dark thoughts, she was still in a romantic comedy. Part of the fun of love affairs was that they were supposed to be furtive, and hadn't even Nora Ephron made Tom Hanks and Meg Ryan seem sneaky when she turned them into e-lovers in *You've Got Mail*? This observation calmed her, at least until she got halfway across the room and suddenly thought *love affair*? The whole point of this was that it was supposed to be a substitute for a genuine romance, a way of exercising her erotic imagination without the hassle of actually betraying her boyfriend.

She sat down on his settee, looking at the TV set-up. The nostalgic romantic in her was pleased to see no sign of a DVD player, and she wondered what tape was sticking out of the video-recorder. She tried to turn the TV on with the remote, before realising it wasn't plugged in. She pushed the tape into the machine, checked the counter and flicked through to the video channel.

Becca wasn't surprised to see Chris had been watching a home movie. What did throw her was that the woman who appeared on the television screen was the dark-haired actress, Diana, who had so impressed James at Scarlett's party. Sitting back on the settee, she tried to work out what was going on. It looked like some sort of audition tape, with the actress reading out scenes from various books.

Every now and again she'd corpse, or nod and close her eyes, or simply get distracted. Looking up, she'd talk to someone off-camera, but her eyes would remain trained on the lens. Her hair was styled differently than it had been at the party, and her green eyes were even more bewitching. It seemed obvious that she'd soon become one of those English actresses whose sexual habits preoccupy everyone.

Becca sat there longer than she'd intended, only getting bored when Diana started doing Maggie the Cat in a preposterous Southern accent. Then she fast-forwarded until the image changed to a shot of Chris in bed. He was bare-chested, and probably naked, although his bottom half was hidden by a fluffy white duvet. He had a bad case of bed-head and a lightly stubbled chin. One hand was outstretched in protest at the camera. Concerned about witnessing something illicit, Becca stopped the tape. She waited a moment, and then pressed play again.

'Are you ready for your close-up?' she heard Diana's voice say as she zoomed in on his chest.

'No,' he said, 'I'm tired. Let me go back to sleep.'

She zoomed out. 'OK, that's fine, I'll film you sleeping.'

He exhaled and lay back on the bed. 'Give me the camera.'

'No,' she said, giggling, 'you always have the camera.'

'Well, turn it off for a moment. Let me get dressed.'

'Relax, don't worry, you look beautiful.'

He smiled. 'And who are you recording this for exactly? Something to show your parents?'

'It's not to show anyone. It's just for me. Now, come on, talk . . .'

'I don't feel like talking.'

'OK,' she said, 'I'll ask you questions.'

Chris closed his eyes. 'What d'you want to know?'

The screen filled with fuzz. Becca was surprised at the abrupt edit and fast-forwarded, searching for more. But the rest of the tape was blank, so she rewound it and froze a still of Chris in bed. It seemed odd to be able to see him like this. The extreme intimacy seemed unearned, and for the first time she felt guilty. At the same time, she felt intrigued and aroused by Chris and Diana's relationship. There seemed something more adult and sexy about the videotaped interplay than anything she'd done with James. She briefly wondered how he'd react if she brought a camera into their bedroom, but found she couldn't imagine it.

Becca stared at Chris's body, still confused about whether she found him attractive. Not that she'd be able to answer if someone asked her what it was that made her fall for James. Yet even if this was only a pretend, unrealised affair, she wanted to make sure he was crush-worthy. Seeing him on tape cleared things up in a way, making him like an actor in a serial who she could take or leave depending on her whim.

Becca couldn't understand why her key failed to slot into the lock. Rather than check it, she pressed harder, jiggling it vigorously back and forth. When this failed, she realised with a start that she'd been trying to open the door with the key to Chris's flat.

James opened it for her.

'What's wrong with your key?'

'Nothing,' she replied too quickly.

'But you were bashing away at the lock like a mad thing. I thought it was someone trying to break in.'

'What are you doing home?'

'I thought I'd surprise you.'

Becca followed James inside, trying to control her anger. She'd clearly done something to make him suspicious, and didn't want to give him further reason to suspect her.

'So where have you been?'

'I know I'm not supposed to go out, but I was going stir-crazy. And there's the ansaphone if any calls did come through.'

'Relax, Becca, I understand. But it's a good job I was here.'

'Why?'

'Because,' he smirked, 'a call did come through.'

'What?'

'ColourMePink Productions.'

'Who?'

He laughed. 'Remember Diana? That girl from the party you didn't think much of?'

'Of course.'

'Well, she put in a good word for you. They had someone who wasn't working out, so . . .'

'As a producer?'

'What?'

'Do they want me to work as a producer?'

'Diana said the job would be a little lower down the ladder than you're used to, but she also told me to remind you that it is for terrestrial television.'

'Channel Five.'

'Yeah, but it's not as if you're inundated with other offers.'

'Thanks for reminding me.'

'I thought you'd be pleased. You said not having a job was getting to you.'

Becca hung up her coat and walked through to the kitchen. She poured herself a glass of water and rubbed her forehead, trying to process this.

'You seem angry,' said James.

'I just hate feeling that people are patronising me.'

'Look, Becca, it's nothing to do with me.'

'I'm not saying it is.'

'Well, what then? Did you really hate that woman that much?'

'No, I didn't hate her. But I have to be so careful. If word gets round that I'm doing this sort of job, people are going to start thinking I'm in trouble.'

'So you're telling me it's better for you to be unemployed than do this job.'

'Maybe, yeah.'

'That's ridiculous.'

Becca slammed the glass down on the kitchen top. 'Right, so I'm being ridiculous. Obviously you and Diana know what's best for me.'

James looked shocked. He moved towards her, palms outwards. 'Look, if you don't want the job, don't take it.'

'And then you'll be angry with me.'

'Don't be silly. Obviously this is important to you, and you're probably right. Maybe it is something I don't understand.'

'James . . .'

'No, stop. Look, I wrote the details and the number down by the phone. Just call her and say thanks, but no thanks.'

Becca sat down. James looked at her.

'Well? Aren't you going to do it?'

'Not right now, no.'

'But you will call?'

'Of course I'll fucking call. Why does it matter to you?'

'I just think that this woman's obviously gone to some trouble for you, and you should say thanks. Besides, they could be relying on you.'

Becca knew she was being unfair. She also knew that while it was conceivable that taking a low-level job could send out the wrong impression, Diana was right, and the fact that it was terrestrial would more than make up for it. She also knew that had she been offered the job two weeks ago she would've accepted immediately.

James left Becca alone and went through to the bedroom. She picked up the remote and turned on the TV, kicked off her shoes and sank her toes into the carpet. For some reason, she suddenly began to feel a whole lot calmer.

Becca's Dodgy Boyfriends #2
Jerry

Among the videos Becca had been watching a little too obsessively recently was *The Man Who Fell to Earth*. She'd first watched it years ago and not really thought that much of it. But two months ago she went with James to the 333 and saw it projected onto the wall. It was hard to tell without the soundtrack, but it seemed better than she remembered and next time she was in HMV she picked up a copy of the tape.

Becca identified with Bowie's earth girlfriend, Mary-Lou. Although she occasionally came across as a little bubble-headed, Becca admired the way she pushed the emotionally absent Bowie into a relationship, especially as all he wanted was to watch his multiple banks of TVs. This had a special resonance for Becca, as by far the weirdest of her previous boyfriends was a guy called Jerry who filled her flat with hundreds of malfunctioning tellies that he intended one day to fix.

Becca and Jerry were together for six months. They broke up over the TVs. Becca told Jerry that she couldn't carry on living surrounded by so many blank screens and asked him to make a choice between his televisions and her.

He left the next morning.

One of the most popular features on Andy's TV show was a section where he talked about how many minutes of a film he'd watched before needing the toilet. It was a slight, vulgar joke, but it'd remained part of his routine since he'd worked on radio. He also had a recurring weekly section where he discussed cinetiquette. Chris's favourite of Andy's rules was that five minutes should be allowed to pass after a film had ended before anyone said anything critical about it. That way they both got to form their opinion before the inevitable argument.

Tonight Andy broke his own rule, turning to Chris the moment the end-credits started rolling.

'That was terrible.'

Chris chuckled. 'At least it wasn't boring.'

'Boring? It gave me a migraine.'

'That's just the polarised photography. It's supposed to have that effect.'

'Why would anyone want to make a film that makes you feel sick? It's so mean-spirited.'

Someone in the row behind them laughed. Chris stood up and took his coat from the back of the chair.

'You said you wanted to see something arty.'

'I said I wanted to see something I hadn't seen already. You decided that meant something arty.'

'What else could it be? You've seen everything mainstream.'

'I don't know . . . I thought you said you knew someone who thought it was good.'

'I do. My friend said it was incredible.'

'Never introduce me to your friend. Come on, let's get a drink before the bar closes.'

They'd been watching *Liquid Sky* in the small screen at the ICA, and Chris welcomed the chance to get the blood back into his limbs. The pins and needles had started half an hour into the film, and he still felt his legs no longer belonged to him as he hobbled behind Andy towards the bar.

'How come you're so cheerful tonight anyway?' Andy asked once he'd bought the drinks and they slid into a space at a table. 'Did you finally get it together with someone?'

Chris shook his head. 'There's no one.'

'No one at all?' he asked. 'Not even a potential new girl?'

'No.'

'What happened on Saturday?'

'What d'you mean?'

'How come you showed up so late?'

'It wasn't that late. I didn't expect you to have gone.'

'Sorry about that.'

'That's OK. I heard you left with the make-up lady.'

'The sound engineer.'

'A one-off?'

'I think so. I gave her my number, but she hasn't called.'

Chris nodded. 'I'm seeing Scarlett on Monday.'

'Yeah?'

'Yeah. We're going to a screening at the Raindance Festival.'

Andy looked up, interested. 'Of what?'

'Do you remember her American friend, Bob?'

'Bob who?'

'Bob Game. He's made this film called *Trust Fund*. It's about a rich American kid spending a summer in Notting Hill. I can't imagine it's going to be especially good, but Scarlett wants to go.'

'Desperate for connections, I expect. What time's the screening?'

'Two. D'you want to come?'

'I'm recording the show Monday. But let me know if you think it's good.'

'OK.'

Andy looked at his watch. 'I guess I'd better give my brother a ring.'

'Quick one before we go?'

Andy nodded, taking his mobile from his inside pocket and turning it on. Chris got up from his seat and made his way to the bar.

Becca took a seat by the window, waiting for Chris to walk by. She was halfway through her mineral water when he appeared. She finished it in two swallows, giving him a chance to get down to the end of the street before following him.

As usual, Becca preferred to see her behaviour as essentially innocent, and certainly didn't consider what she was doing to be anything as serious as stalking. As far as she was concerned, she was simply a kooky young heroine. Di Keaton in the seventies. A pre sell-out Winona. Ellen DeGeneres if she'd stayed in the closet. Meg Ryan in one of her more risky romantic roles. Maybe Parker Posey if she'd continued her move into the mainstream and had a sympathetic screen-writer. Becca smiled to herself, pleased to have imagined herself in such good company.

Chris went into a newsagent just before he reached the station. Becca responded by ducking down a side street. She knew she was probably over-reacting, but thought that was better than blowing things this early. She was surprised how easy it was to follow someone. This made her wonder if anyone had ever followed her, and she enjoyed one of those odd moments like you get at the end of most conspiracy thrillers where the twist is that the person doing the watching is being watched by someone else, and so on and so on until it all extends out to an odd graphic suggesting an endless chain of observation all the way out to another planet.

He came out of the newsagent with a copy of the *Standard* and a can of Coke and Becca resumed her pursuit.

The station was the first tricky bit. It was shaped so passengers had a clear view of the entrance until they went down on the escalators to the lower level. Downstairs, a train arrived roughly every other minute, which meant that Becca had to stay out of the station until Chris was going down on the escalator, but then had to be right behind him as he made his way to the train. A minute wrong either side and everything would be ruined.

She did, at least, already have a tube ticket, which made following him quickly less of a problem. Gauging how long it'd take him to get to the escalators was more difficult. Then as Chris went through the front entrance, the solution came to her.

Connected to the front of the tube station was a small key-cutting and heel replacement booth. If she stood slightly to the left of the heel machine and the stacks of broken shoes, it was possible to observe the ticket machines and windows without being in view. Becca slipped a non-essential key from her Pink Panther fob and joined the back of the queue.

There were three people in front of her. The first guy was a dishevelled tramp. He had a short ginger beard and was wearing a holey black top over a pair of stained jeans. He held his overcoat over his left shoulder. In his other hand was a trainer that looked as useless as a burst tyre. His foot was bare and extremely black.

'I really don't think I'm going to be able to mend that shoe,' the attendant told him. After thirty seconds, the tramp shrugged and moved on.

Chris seemed to be having some problems with the ticket machine and had joined the back of the queue to the ticket office instead. The ticket queue was going down quickly and Chris was soon served. Becca put the key back into her pocket and moved round towards the front entrance, waiting until

Chris's head disappeared down past the metal of the escalators before heading across.

She looked quickly to the display. One minute until the next train. She fed her ticket through the gates. The tramp was in front of her on the escalator, still carrying his useless shoe. When she was at the top, Chris was at the bottom, although there were enough people between them to obscure his vision of her.

The tube whistled into the station at just the right moment. Chris boarded one of the first carriages and Becca boarded an adjoining one, still stuck behind the tramp. The doors closed behind her and the tube left the station.

Chris got off at Piccadilly Circus. Becca waited until he was almost out of sight and then nipped out onto the platform and went after him. Keeping close to the wall, she followed him to the escalators and took the first step as he was halfway up, tilting her head down in case he looked over his shoulder. In the short time she'd been following Chris she'd noticed he often looked over his shoulder, almost as if he was expecting to be followed.

She followed him the short distance to Rupert Street, then waited as he went into the Metro. When it was clear he wasn't coming out, she walked across to the cinema and went up to the counter.

'Can I have a ticket, please?'

'For what?'

'What just went in?'

'*Trust Fund.*'

'OK, I'll have one for that.'

'It's sold out.'

'Really?'

'I'm sorry, it's because of the Festival. Most of the screenings are sold out.'

'Is the bar still open?'

'Yes. But you have to buy a ticket.'

'OK. What's on after *Trust Fund*?'

'*Hamsters*.'

'*Hamsters*? Is that a nature film?'

'No, it's sci-fi. You can read the review there.' She pointed to the board. Next to the printed review was a photograph of a giant hamster with three shadowy figures running away into the distance.

'It's OK, just give me one ticket.'

'For *Hamsters*?' she asked, announcing the title with relish.

'Yes,' Becca replied, digging into her pocket for change.

The woman printed out a ticket and gave it to Becca, who walked back out into the street. She looked up the road to Raymond's Revue Bar and then went in the opposite direction, wondering how best to kill these next ninety minutes.

She decided not to head to her usual spots, but to get lunch instead, going for a sandwich at a Pret a Manger. She tried to eat slowly, keen to kill time, but within a few minutes she'd polished off the food and drained her Diet Coke. She picked up her Waterstone's bag and took out the prop, wondering if it was worth reading. She couldn't remember the last time she'd read anything more than a few years old, and she wondered whether James would feel intimidated by the sight of an Oxford World's Classic on her side of the bed.

Becca left the sandwich shop and walked back up towards the cinema. When she reached the Metro, the woman smiled at her as she went down to the bar. Becca bought a Budvar from the Spanish man serving and sat at one of the padded red leather stools that were bolted into the floor. She opened her book and began reading.

*

Becca smiled at Chris. He was the third or fourth person leaving the screen and spotted her immediately. She felt giddy as he smiled back and strode towards her. She put one hand over the page she was reading, ready to utter her line.

Then she saw Scarlett.

'Becca,' she cried, moving past Chris and embracing her, 'were you watching the film? What did you think? Isn't Stephen fabulous? I mean, the true genius lies in Bob's direction, but Stephen, my God. Did you hear he's working with Gwyneth next?'

Becca looked at Scarlett, up at Chris, and then back to Scarlett. She knew she should tell them that she hadn't been at the screening, but also that if she did so, she'd have to tell them she had a ticket for the film about to go in. She also wanted to know whether there was anything between Chris and Scarlett.

Scarlett stepped back. 'So do you two know each other?'

'No,' said Becca, offering her hand.

'Becca, this is Chris. Chris, Becca.'

They shook hands. Chris looked at the people filing out.

'Is anything happening afterwards?'

'I don't think so. But what about you guys? You want to do something? Shall we all go for a drink?'

Becca looked at Chris, holding her breath.

'Sure,' he said, 'why not?'

'Well,' said Scarlett, as if he'd suddenly reminded her of something, 'I can't stay too long, but I could manage a couple of rounds.'

'So where shall we go?'

'Well, you know what, shall we just go to Soho House?'

Becca looked at Chris, curious whether he would raise an objection, but he just shrugged and they set off.

'So, are you working on this?' Scarlett asked, picking up Becca's copy of *The Mayor of Casterbridge* and flicking through it.

'What?' she asked, confused.

'Who's doing it? Is it a FilmFour thing?'

'Oh, I see. No, I'm just reading it.'

'Yeah, yeah, so it's secret, is that what you're saying? Don't worry, I don't know anyone who does heritage stuff.'

'It's a good idea to do another Hardy,' said Chris, although his tone was unenthusiastic, 'after all, you're guaranteed the A-level audience. There was that one they made simply because it was on the syllabus.'

'*Jude*.'

'No, no, the Scarlet something. It was based on one of the short stories.'

'Are you sure?'

'I think so. *The Scarlet Tunic*, was it?'

Scarlett nodded. 'Well, if his stories are being made into films, it makes perfect sense to do one of the novels. Although you'd need someone like Eccleston playing the lead.'

Becca stared at the pair of them, amazed at how quickly the conversation had spun out of control. No doubt by next week there'd be three new Hardy adaptations in production. Becca wanted to tell them why she'd really brought the book, just to see how they'd react, but knew that if she did so she'd scare off Chris and probably lose Scarlett's friendship.

'So,' Scarlett smiled at Chris, 'what are you working on at the moment?'

Chris chuckled. 'I'm embarrassed to tell you.'

'God, you're both so bloody coy,' said Scarlett, frowning. 'Do you think I'll steal your ideas as well?'

'No,' said Chris, 'it's not that. I'm genuinely embarrassed about it.'

Becca liked the way Chris clutched the back of his neck as he said this, and felt excited all over again. He leaned back and brushed his fringe from his eyes.

'You big tease,' Scarlett scolded, then she asked, 'Is it something you're embarrassed about because you're only doing it for the money?'

'Exactly the opposite. It's a labour of love.'

'You're writing a novel?'

'No,' he laughed, 'why does everyone think that? It's non-fiction.'

'So it is a book?'

'I don't know if it's anything. It's a project.'

Scarlett smiled. 'I've got one of those. It's something I do when I get bogged down in the other stuff. Sort of a glamorised video-diary.'

Chris looked at Becca. 'And what about you, Becca? Do you have a secret project?'

James was waiting for her when she got home. Bracing herself for another argument, she walked up behind his chair and leaned down to kiss him.

'Hi,' she said.

He smiled. 'Another film?'

'Preview. I went with Scarlett.'

He didn't reply. She leaned down to check his expression, and realised this wasn't an angry silence, but a defensive one. It was clear he wasn't up for an argument any more than she was, making her feel relieved and grateful. She moved round and sat on his lap. They both watched the TV for a moment, James stroking her hair.

'Did you call Diana?' he asked.

She shook her head. 'I tried, but I couldn't get through. I'll give it another go tomorrow.'

He smiled and kissed her. Previously, Becca had no intention of calling that woman, no matter what she'd told James. But after seeing her on the video, she thought it might be interesting. It was much easier to think of Chris as a research subject than a prospective boyfriend, and this would be a good way of gathering fresh information. Pleased with this new plan, she kissed James again, moved off his lap and walked through to the bedroom.

'So you all found it boring?'

Chris looked round at his class, fearing that his planned lesson was about to go down the toilet. Surely someone had something to say: even something slight would get things going. He scanned their faces. It was Nadine, his favourite student, who came to the rescue.

'I found it quite boring when we were watching it, but then when you told us to think about the film for the next lesson I thought of some things to say about it.'

Chris was touched by her faith. He had to concede it was a mistake to show this class *The Passenger*. Certain films worked differently with different groups, and it was lazy of him to bash through the same movies every year. And it wasn't as if there was any real logic to his selection: when he started teaching he'd been told to hand in a list of films to put in the Lomax Centre Prospectus, and he'd stuck with the same titles ever since.

'OK, Nadine, go on.'

She looked round at the others, obviously aware that what she was about to say would prompt dissent. 'Well, my thoughts were more about Jack Nicholson than Antonioni.'

'That's OK. Tell us what you came up with.'

'Well, I was mainly thinking about how Jack Nicholson is the most famous film star in the world . . .'

She tailed off as the various factions of the class began to murmur their disagreement. For the mad old men, the most famous film star was Marlon Brando. For the Sunday-supplement gang, it was Will Smith. The Taranteenies pitched in with De Niro. Someone at the back suggested Tom Cruise. But Chris homed in on Nadine, saying,

'I think you've got a good point. Certainly Jack doesn't carry the weird baggage of Brando, and across the board he's probably better known than De Niro. So . . .'

'Well, I was just wondering how he reached that position.'

'I think everyone in Hollywood would like to know the answer to that, Nadine.'

'No, what I mean is, I know he's famous now because of his image, but which came first? The notoriety or the acclaim? And isn't it interesting that the only time he's worked with really top-notch directors, they've been Europeans like Polanski or Antonioni . . . apart from Kubrick, I suppose, but usually Jack works with second-rate talents, like Milos Forman or Tim Burton.'

She looked to Chris for approval. He could sense the class gearing up for an argument, and gratefully smiled at his saviour.

After the class, Chris felt more drained than usual and couldn't face the pub. He caught the last bus home and walked the last few hundred yards to his flat. He felt slightly nervous as he opened the door, scared he might find a burglar inside. He'd been feeling a bit freaked recently, constantly imagining that things in his flat weren't always the same way he left them when he returned. He took off his jacket, sat down and picked up the phone. Then he reached for his address book and dialled.

'Hello?'

'Hi, Scarlett, it's Chris here.'

'Hi, Chris. Can I call you back? I'm in the middle of dinner.'

'Sure, but look, it's something really quick.'

'Oh, OK, what's up?'

'That woman we met on Monday.'

'Becca.'

'Is she seeing anyone?'

Scarlett laughed. 'I knew you liked her. Well, look, she's going out with a guy called James, but between you and me, I don't think things are going that well. At my party he got really drunk and was all over . . .'

'Who?'

'No, shit, listen, I wasn't thinking. Forget I said anything.'

'What? Come on, Scarlett, tell me. It could be important.'

'Look, don't get upset, Chris, but it was Diana. He was all over Diana.'

Chris didn't reply.

'Chris?' Scarlett asked. 'Listen, I'm sure nothing's going to happen between James and Diana. I only said it so you'd know that, well, it's not a rock-solid relationship.'

He looked round his room, imagining Scarlett on the other end of the line, eating dinner. So Becca's boyfriend was interested in Diana. He told himself this was a good thing, but found he still felt jealous.

'Chris . . .'

'I'm sorry, I should let you get back to your food.'

'Yeah,' she said, then after a pause, 'Actually, Chris, I've got an idea. A friend of mine is trying to get a group together to go to this thing at the Prince Charles.'

'Not SingalongaSoundofMusic?'

'What? No. It's Twelve Hour Teens, an all-night screening of *Heathers, Ferris Bueller, Pretty in Pink*.'

His heart sank. 'God, no.'

'What?'

'I've seen all those films a hundred times. I don't think I

could watch one of them once more, let alone sit through an all-night screening.'

'It's not just the old ones, there's new stuff as well . . . *She's All That, Never Been Kissed.*'

'They're even worse. At least the first time round teen films were a legitimate guilty pleasure. Now you get Andy's mates writing about the sexual politics of *American Pie* in *Sight and Sound.*'

'No, wait, I haven't told you the best part.'

'What? We have to dress up as our favourite characters?'

'Um . . . yeah.'

Chris laughed. 'Sorry, no, I'm not doing it.'

'But, look, I'll bring Becca with me. And you can bring Andy and we'll fix it so your characters match.'

'Have you asked Becca?'

'No, not yet. But if I do, will you consider it?'

'If Becca agrees to go, then yes, I'll consider it.'

Becca sat on the sofa with James, watching *The Newton Boys*. The film was not one she would've chosen under normal circumstances (it was another rainy-day title), but she'd felt hurried and it was one of the few tapes in which James had expressed an interest. So she'd let him rent it, foolishly thinking that she should be being nice to him, and now she was sitting here hating it, and feeling really anxious about what he had planned for the remainder of the evening.

It wasn't the movie. She'd always liked Richard Linklater, and couldn't understand why this film hadn't been given a theatrical release in England. It seemed jaunty enough, and the four stars were charismatic, especially Ethan Hawke. She supposed it was to do with the cyclical trend of westerns becoming fashionable and unfashionable again, although it could also be down to disappointment that a director who in his first three films had spoken so clearly to Generation X had sought refuge in a genre piece.

No, it wasn't the movie. It was more the reality of sitting here with James, neither of them really content but unable to come up with anything else they'd rather do instead. She felt like she was in a soap or a sit-com, going through a scene that was needed for the story but had no real point.

She wondered if things would be different if they'd gone to the cinema. She'd probably still be thinking the same things, but maybe the excitement of the cinema ritual (something she still felt every single trip, especially at evening screenings) would have romanticised her situation. Soap opera characters didn't tend to go to the cinema, maybe because to introduce a regular period of reflection would stop their heads overheating and maim the melodramatic flow. Movie characters didn't tend to go to the cinema that much either (although there were honourable exceptions, like the guy in *The Goalkeeper's Fear of the Penalty*). Characters in books also didn't go, which struck Becca as strange, especially as nineteenth-century novelists had got so much mileage out of characters going to the theatre or the opera in times of turmoil.

James picked up that she wasn't watching the film with her usual interest and pressed pause.

'What's wrong?'

'I'm sorry. I'm finding it hard to concentrate.'

'Do you want me to stop it?'

The phone rang.

'No, you carry on watching it. I'll get that.'

'OK.'

Becca stood up and went out into the hallway, picking up the receiver.

'Hello?'

'Hi, Becca, it's Scarlett.'

'Hi.'

'Is this a good time?'

'What for?'

'Is James there?'

'Yeah.' She lowered her voice. 'In the other room. Why?'

'No reason. I'll tell you some other time. The reason I'm calling is, well, what are you doing next Friday night?'

'Why do I have to be Emilio Estevez?'

'Because that's the whole point. Scarlett's getting Becca to dress up as Molly Ringwald and she's going as Ally Sheedy.'

'And?'

'Molly Ringwald ends up with Judd Nelson.' Chris looked at Andy, waiting to see if he'd accept this logic.

'Don't you think this is all a little bit . . .'

'What?'

'Stupid?'

'Yes. And I expect Becca thinks it's stupid too. But it might be just the thing to convince her to break up with her boyfriend and go out with me. And who knows, maybe something'll happen between you and Scarlett.'

'I don't want anything to happen between me and Scarlett. I don't fancy Scarlett.'

'How can you not fancy Scarlett? Everyone fancies Scarlett. Besides, you owe this to me.'

'How d'you work that out?'

'Claudia.'

'What?'

'Remember that time when she made you go to that black tie dinner and you needed someone to come along and be a date for her friend?'

'That was ten years ago.'

'So?'

The tube reached their stop. Andy got up and went through the open doors. Chris followed him.

'Do you remember Nancy Travis?'

'From *Three Men and a Little Lady*?'

'No, shit, not Travis, what was she called. Lucas. Nancy Lucas.'

'No.'

'You do. From junior school.'

Chris stared at his friend, astounded at this latest leap. 'Right . . .'

'And do you remember her friend Beth?'

'I think so. Why?'

'I never told you this before, but I had a big crush on Beth and I told Nancy and she said that Beth thought I was OK but wouldn't go out with me because I was too scruffy. And so I told Nancy to tell Beth that if she agreed to be my girlfriend I wouldn't be scruffy any more. Only Nancy said that wasn't good enough and told me that if I wanted to go out with Beth I had to go through a sort of initiation test.'

'Are you making this up?'

'No, listen, this was a very emotional moment for me.'

'OK. Go on.'

'Alright. The test was that the following Friday I had to come in as smart as possible, and if I scored ten out of ten from Nancy and her two friends, then I could go out with Beth. So I went home and I even told my parents and they bought me new clothes and let me have a bath even though it wasn't my bath night and I went in the next day and the first girl looked at me and she gave me a ten, and then the second girl looked at me and she also gave me a ten, and then Nancy looked at me and said she was sorry but she could only give me nine and a half. And when I asked why she said it was because I'd brought Beth the wrong kind of flowers.'

'That's terrible.'

'I know.'

'But what's your point?'

'The point is, that's what girls are like. If I'd brought the right kind of flowers she would've found some other reason for disqualifying me. Maybe she would've said that I'd parted my hair on the wrong side. Or that I was wearing the wrong colour shoelaces. Beth didn't want to go out with me. It was a set-up.'

'And?'

'And that's what this thing sounds like.'

'You think Scarlett's going to stop me going out with Becca because I've got the wrong colour shoelaces?'

'I don't know. But there's something funny about it.'

'You're insane.'

They walked out onto the street.

'That's why you're always smart, isn't it?' Chris asked Andy, turning on him. 'Because of that thing that happened to you when you were a kid.'

'Where are we going?'

'First Sport.'

'Why?'

'To get you some jock clothes. I bet you haven't worn trainers in years.'

Chris's Favourite Films #45
In the Mouth of Madness

Chris was more interested in the idea of horror films than the reality. He'd always been fascinated by the concept of sequels, and loved the fact that there were at least ten *Friday the 13th* films without feeling the need to watch them. He did buy the tapes occasionally, satisfying the collector urge in him. He also genuinely liked the *Scream* trilogy and a few others of the latest revival of horror movies. But his favourite horror film hardly counted as a horror film at all.

In the Mouth of Madness only had a fifteen certificate, and to Chris's concern, only seemed to work its magic on excessive drug addicts or the already unhinged. The fact that it also terrified him could, he thought, be put down to his overactive imagination, although when he'd first gone to see it with Andy at a midnight screening, his friend had been equally terrified, so maybe it had something to do with seeing it in the cinema.

The most frightening bit of the film for him was a tiny moment of quiet spookiness. Sam Neill is driving along a silent, deserted street when he notices a shadowy figure cycling behind him. The two of them get involved in a duel for the road, but what Chris found especially scary was the sound of the cyclist's wheel. He has a small card placed to click against his spokes and for a brief moment that's the only thing audible. Walking back from the cinema after the movie, Chris and Andy heard a cycle behind them making this same noise and ran home as fast as they could.

Becca stood by the telephone, half-dressed and beginning to feel awkward. Her feet and ankles were cold, and a particularly vicious draught was beginning to sweep up her legs. She wanted to put the phone down and rush to the bathroom for the rest of her clothes, but a misguided sense of politeness kept her waiting while Diana talked to someone else, her audible conversation irritatingly inconsequential.

'Sorry about that, Becca,' her voice said, suddenly clear over the background noise. 'I'm going to have to get back in a minute.'

'That's OK,' she replied. 'I just wanted to fix up a time for a proper meeting.'

'So you are interested?' Diana asked, clearly surprised.

'Well, I'd like to have a chat first. But maybe, yeah.'

'OK, the thing is, though, Becca, there isn't really that much time for you to make up your mind. We'd need a decision almost straight away.'

'So there wouldn't be time for us to meet up?'

'Not really. And to be honest, I'm not really the person you should meet. Why don't you call Brian at ColourMePink? Do you have his number?'

'Yeah, you gave it to James. But I just wondered, could we meet up anyway?'

'Like for a drink, or something?'

'If that's OK with you.'

'Well, I am horrendously busy, but I suppose I probably could manage it. When did you have in mind?'

Becca arrived late, expecting Diana to keep her waiting. But she was already at the bar, drinking from a full glass. She didn't notice Becca until she'd taken the stool alongside her, and then only said quietly,

'Hi.'

'Sorry I'm late. I had a phone call just as I was coming out. Actually . . .' She smiled at Diana and went in for the kill. 'It was a friend of yours.'

'Really? Who?'

'Um . . . Chris.'

Diana sat up, and looked suspicious. Becca had spent a long time deciding on her technique for this evening. She knew she was probably more intimidated by Diana than the woman merited, but every time she'd rehearsed this meeting she imagined that Diana would get the upper hand by leaving before she had a chance to initiate a proper conversation. So she'd decided to start tough and slowly back off, getting her attention but not being so obnoxious that Diana would leave. That way she could get maximum information out of her in minimum time, and judge her personality by how she tolerated her aggressiveness.

'Chris Paley?'

She nodded. 'I met him the other day.'

'At Scarlett's party?'

'No, at a screening. Bob Game's film.'

'Oh,' said Diana, sipping her drink, 'did you go to that?'

Becca hesitated, and then realised it was safest to lie. 'Yeah.' She nodded. 'How was it?'

'Not bad.'

Diana leaned back. 'Was it like his shorts?'

'Um . . . more of a comedy.'

'Really?' she said. 'Don't you think some of those shorts are hilarious?'

'Well, yeah, but this . . .'

'What's your favourite?'

'Pardon?'

'Bob's shorts. Which one's your favourite?'

She hesitated. 'I think they're all pretty good. It's hard to pick an absolute favourite. I don't know, which one do you like?'

'*Mercy Killing*, that's my favourite. I love that actress who plays the vet's assistant. I don't know why he doesn't use her more. You know she's just a girl from his home town who had no ambition to be an actress? She won't work at all unless Bob uses her, and then he doesn't . . . I don't know, who's in this film?'

'New people, except for Stephen.'

'Mackintosh?'

'No, not him . . . he's working with Gwyneth Paltrow next.'

'Bob?'

'No, Stephen . . . damn, you know how it is when you forget an actor's name?'

'Don't worry, I'm sure it'll come back to you. But who else is in it? Run through the names, I'm sure I'll know most of them.'

'They're all unknowns. Sorry, I'm crap with names.'

'That's OK. Anyway, how well do you know Chris?'

'Not very.'

'But you know I went out with him?'

'God, no, I didn't know that. Sorry, I feel like an idiot. Was that recently?'

'Actually,' Diana said wistfully, 'we just broke up.'

'Really? I feel so stupid. I'm sorry for bringing him up. It's just, I don't really know you very well and I was pleased to find a connection. I'm sorry, I feel so gauche.'

Diana turned round, her posture less defensive. Clearly

enjoying Becca's elaborate apologies, she finished her drink at the same moment the bartender finally came across to serve Becca.

'Can I get you another . . . ?'

'Vodka tonic, thanks.'

Becca ordered the drinks and put her elbows on top of the bar. Diana looked at her.

'It's OK,' she said, 'I'm over Chris. I thought it would take longer, and it probably would have done if I didn't have this part, but my character's emotional life is so intense I hardly have room for my own thoughts. And if I do feel depressed, it's actually really useful. Last night I started crying when I remembered something, and instead of, like, giving in to it, I got my dictaphone and recorded myself. Actually,' she looked around and took a small tape-recorder from her pocket, 'would you mind if I taped this conversation?'

Diana turned her face towards her, smiling encouragingly. Becca wondered for a moment whether she was being set up. Her recent sneakiness had made her suspicious about the motivations of others, and she suddenly thought that maybe Chris had cottoned on to what she was up to and launched a counter-attack, roping in his ex-girlfriend to make it seem convincing.

'It would just be really useful research for me. I know this sounds silly, but while I was going out with Chris I got really depressed and didn't see my female friends as much as I used to . . . well, there were one or two, Annabel, I stayed in contact with her, she's my best friend . . . and I saw groups of people, but I didn't really go out in this friendly way, you know what I mean?'

Becca nodded. 'Things get like that with James sometimes.'

'James is your boyfriend?'

'Yeah, you remember, you met him at the party.'

She looked away. 'Right. So you stop seeing your friends sometimes when you're in a couple?'

Diana's questions made Becca feel like she was being interviewed. She wanted to find a way to turn the conversation back to Diana, but at the same time didn't want to encourage her to start droning on about her programme again. She could feel her control of the evening slipping away from her, and wondered if she should be rude again. But it was hard to find another opening. Becca realised Diana was waiting for her to respond.

'God,' she said, 'I hardly see anyone when I'm not working. Scarlett's party was the first time I'd been out socially in ages.'

'She's good at that, Scarlett, isn't she? Although . . . I suppose I shouldn't really say this, but I sometimes get the impression that she doesn't really like me.' Diana picked up the dictaphone and rewound it back. 'Sorry.' She smiled. 'I don't want to hear myself saying that on tape.'

'I know what you mean. I think she forgets about me. She's one of these people who has so many friends she doesn't worry if there's some she doesn't see for a while. She's lucky like that. But I suppose it's the nature of the business. I hardly see anyone when I'm working on a show, and then when a job comes to an end and I want some friends to go out with, they're never around any more.'

'I know,' Diana said. 'It's like that being an actress, only much, much worse. You have all that job stuff, but then there's all these other complications like sometimes one of your friends becomes much more famous than you, and it's really hard for the relationship to balance. Or sometimes you make really close friends on a film set, and then when the movie's over you never see those people again . . . although I suppose I haven't really experienced anything like that yet.'

Becca looked at Diana, still uncertain what she thought of

her. She was egotistical and self-obsessed, but that was clearly something she was trying to cultivate, and probably necessary in her industry if she was going to have any success. She'd been a little worried when Diana mentioned how she'd been depressed with Chris, but it wasn't as if she was implying that it was his fault, and even if that was what she was saying, Diana might have sensed her interest in Chris and adopted this strategy to put her off.

'It's weird, actually, because Pamela . . . that's my character in the series . . . isn't really the social type either, but, and this is a bit embarrassing, but the reason I wanted to tape us is that in the first couple of episodes I'm making friends with this woman called Amber . . .'

'The bisexual character.'

'You remembered that? Wow. Yeah, well, before Amber makes a pass at me, the two of them have lots of scenes where they're out together, just drinking like this and chatting about men. And although we've got these fantastic scripts, the director's got more of a film background and he's really keen for us to improvise. To be honest, I think he'd much rather be making a film, and he's using this TV series sort of as training and also to make his name. Anyway, I've been finding it really difficult to know what I'm going to say in those scenes, so I wondered if you and I could, y'know . . .'

'You want me to come on to you?'

'Oh no,' Diana said quickly, 'no, nothing like that. I just wondered if we could carry on like this, talking about relationships and stuff.'

'OK,' she said, 'tell me what happened with you and Chris.'

'Why we broke up, you mean?'

'Anything, just give me an idea of what the relationship was like.'

'I don't know. Chris is quite an enigmatic man, in a way.

You haven't known him that long so you probably haven't seen much of it, but he can be really strange sometimes. I know that sounds cold, but Chris is someone you can't help having conflicting feelings about. He's very amiable, and extremely kind, but there's something steely there.'

'Steely in what way?'

'It's hard to define. It's like there's two conflicting impulses fighting each other inside him. He has this strong self-belief, but at the same time he's ashamed of those feelings and also worried about trampling on other people . . . and I know it sounds terrible, but I think that's what holds him back. It's a shame he's never wanted to be an actor. I think a lot of that turmoil inside him could be really useful fuel for a performer.'

'My friend Jessica thinks he looks like David Duchovny.'

Diana laughed. 'Really? How does she know him?'

'Oh,' said Becca, suddenly aware that she'd said too much, 'she's his estate agent.'

Becca waited for Diana to start unpicking these tangled connections, but she ignored the challenge, instead asking her if she wanted another drink. Becca nodded, and then asked Diana,

'So how did you meet? Through Scarlett?'

'No, it was at a dinner party. And that sort of fits in with what I'm talking about and how I feel about Chris. The problem with our relationship wasn't really anything to do with either of us . . . it was more the timing. Everything about it was wrong. We never really had things balanced. When he first met me . . . I know this 'cause he told me, and he obviously felt really proud of it . . . he decided that I was going to be this big love in his life, and that was fine because I was single at the time, but he expected me to reciprocate right away. I mean, it wasn't as if I didn't love him or anything, it's just that the whole time we were together he was moving into a really insular stage of his life, and I was the opposite, feeling desperate to get out there and get my career going. I've never really said all this to Chris because he's bound to think it's a big tragedy, when really it's just . . . life.'

Becca nodded. 'A lot of men are like that.'

'Oh, don't get me wrong, he's a lovely person, and if I'd met him at a different time, he probably could've been the love of my life too. Although there was one thing about him that really pissed me off.'

'What?'

'It was just a little thing, but it caused so much tension between us.'

Becca looked at Diana, waiting.

'He didn't like me drinking. Well, not drinking, getting drunk. He hated it when I came home pissed.'

'Did he shout at you?'

'No, Chris isn't really the shouting type. But he'd sulk, and sometimes that was almost more annoying.'

'I can see how that'd be irritating.'

'I suppose, to be fair, he doesn't drink that much himself . . . well, he does, he's not a teetotaller or anything . . . but he gets weird about really going for it. That was annoying, especially after a show when I just wanted to get blasted and celebrate. But, hey, I'm doing all the talking. Why don't you tell me about James?'

Diana smiled, and Becca started talking about her relationship, frankly, but remaining a little more guarded than she'd be with someone like Jessica or Scarlett. It was partly the tape-recorder in front of her that made her reticent, but it was also Diana's manner, and the knowledge that she was trying to fake friendliness. They stayed late in the bar, and when they left Becca felt too drunk to navigate the tube and caught a taxi home instead.

Becca's Dodgy Boyfriends #3
Colin

Becca had never been a big fan of dressing gowns, but she'd given them up completely since Colin, an ex-boyfriend who'd worn one almost all the time he was indoors. Colin was the scuzziest of her former lovers, giving her three nasty cases of cystitis and managing to put her off sex even when she wasn't in pain. He insisted she wore the nasty red towelling robe he'd bought her whenever they were together, referring to their idle afternoons as 'the dressing-gown hours'.

Colin had broken up with Becca to go travelling, telling her he'd be gone so long there was no point trying to maintain a long-distance relationship. Although their sex life hadn't been fantastic, Colin did have a certain charm and Becca was distraught to see him go. When he left, she reminded him to keep her address and phone number, telling him to get in touch when he got back, just in case things had changed.

'You look exactly the same as you always do.'

'It's a new coat,' Chris said, defensively.

'Is it?' Andy asked, fingering the material. 'Where d'you get it?'

'I mean, it's second hand, but I only just bought it.' He looked at Andy, realising he'd only answered one of his questions. 'I got it from a charity shop, why?'

'You don't remember which one?'

'No. It wasn't Oxfam.' He paused. 'Why are you so interested?'

'It's a nice coat.'

Chris smiled. 'Do you think so? I can look for the receipt.'

'Don't bother.' He walked across to the settee. 'Have we got time for a drink?'

'No, but we're meeting everyone else in a bar before the movie.'

'You didn't tell me that.'

'Only because I knew you'd get all precious about going out in your jock outfit.'

'So you knew I'd be upset and arranged it anyway? Thanks a fucking bunch.'

'Look, everyone's going to look stupid.'

'Except for you. You look fine. Give me your coat.'

'What? No. You've got a coat.'

'Let's swap. We can change when we get there.'

'No, I need to get into character.'

Andy snorted, then said, 'What if someone tries to beat me up?'

'Why would anyone want to beat you up?'

'I don't know. People don't like jocks, do they? It reminds them of getting beaten up in high school.'

'Andy, we're in England.'

'I know, but . . .'

'And we're going to the Zoo Bar. I hardly think you're going to be set upon by a gang of marauding geeks.'

A horn sounded outside.

'Who's that?'

'Your brother.'

'He told me he was busy tonight.'

'I know. I told him to say that.'

'Why?'

'You'll understand in a minute.'

Andy didn't say anything, gathering his stuff and following Chris outside. As he got into his brother's taxi and saw how he was dressed everything became clear.

'Oh no,' said Andy quietly. 'How did this happen?'

Andy's brother looked nervous. 'It was Chris's idea. I owed him a favour.'

'Did he buy you those clothes?' Andy asked.

His brother turned round, looking, Chris was happy to note, the spitting image of the film's geekiest character. 'Actually, Andy, most of the stuff I'm wearing is yours.'

'What?' Andy demanded, leaning forward and tugging at his brother's collar. He wriggled uselessly.

'Yeah, don't worry, it's stuff you haven't worn for ages. I found it in a black bag in your old bedroom.'

Chris kept quiet, not wanting to inflame the situation. Andy saw the joke and started laughing. Chris smiled and patted his shoulder, as he sat back and let his brother drive them to the Zoo Bar.

It'd taken Chris a long time to learn how to enjoy these sorts of events. Five years ago, Andy would be the one dragging him along. But during his time with Diana he'd grown more comfortable with enjoying himself, and any adolescent fear of looking stupid had vanished. Admittedly, he would've felt slightly more reluctant if he was wearing Andy's outfit, but that was more to do with a lifelong fear of sports and sportswear than concern about his appearance.

Scarlett had been the one to suggest meeting at the Zoo Bar. She was like that sometimes, as happy in overcrowded pubs as she was in her private members' clubs. Chris had only been to the Zoo Bar once before, and that had been in the afternoon when it was relatively quiet. Andy's brother took ages parking the taxi, and by the time they got inside the bar Scarlett was already waiting with a group of about ten people.

Andy's brother went up to the bar to get the drinks. Chris sat down next to a man wearing dark glasses, a white shirt and boxer shorts.

'Tom Cruise, right? *Risky Business*?'

'Uh, no,' he replied. 'David Arquette in *Never Been Kissed*. The bit where he goes to a fancy dress party dressed as Tom Cruise in *Risky Business*.'

'Clever. Want to guess who I am?'

The woman next to the boxer shorts man leaned across her partner's hairy legs. She was also dressed in her underwear, although covered up by a long raincoat.

'You're John Cusack, aren't you?' she asked.

'Which film?'

'I don't know. *Say Anything*?'

'No, I'm not John Cusack. I'm Judd Nelson.'

'In *The Breakfast Club*?'

Chris nodded, and gestured to Andy. 'He's Emilio, his brother's Anthony Michael Hall, Scarlett's Ally Sheedy, and Becca . . .'

'Isn't here yet,' Scarlett told him, bending down to kiss him. 'James sprung a surprise dinner on her. She's going to come as soon as she can, but it probably won't be until after the first film's started.'

'What's the first film?'

'*Pretty in Pink*.'

Chris looked back at the woman in her underwear. 'Did you tell me who you've come as?'

'Diane Lane.'

'In what?' he asked, surprised.

'*Rumble Fish*. You know the bit where Matt Dillon fantasises about her and she appears on top of a cupboard.'

'Right,' Chris replied, confused. 'Are they showing *Rumble Fish* tonight?'

She shook her head. 'But I couldn't think who else I wanted to be. I don't like teen films that much.'

'Me neither,' he told her.

Andy's brother returned with the drinks. He put them down on the glass-topped table and handed them out. Chris drank a long swallow and looked out the window, feeling disappointed. He didn't want to be sitting here with the underwear couple; he wanted to be getting to know Becca better. And if she'd just been out with her boyfriend she probably wouldn't be in the mood for him to flirt with her. He looked up at Scarlett.

'Are there breaks between the films?'

'No,' she said, 'it's continuous. They've got eight films to get through. But I think it's fine to go out into the auditorium while the films are screening.'

'Or sleep,' said Andy's brother, laughing.

'No,' said Scarlett, lightly patting his head, 'no sleeping.'

He looked up, surprised and pleased by the attention. Scarlett remained standing in the middle of everyone. Smiling at Chris, she asked,

'Shall I do the introductions?'

'OK.'

She ran through the names of the rest of her group. Chris checked out their costumes, but none of them were quite as arresting as the underwear couple. The last people she introduced were two men both dressed as Christian Slater in *Heathers*.

'I did try to make sure we didn't have any doubles.'

'But I changed my mind at the last minute,' explained the second JD. 'Originally I was going to come as a keg of beer, but the costume was too complicated.'

Chris wondered where Scarlett had found these people. He supposed most of them were working on the movie, and he leaned across to shake hands with the man sitting opposite him, who was dressed (Scarlett had explained) as Eric Stoltz in *Some Kind of Wonderful*.

'Sorry,' said Chris, 'I didn't catch your name.'

'Joel,' he replied, blinking twice. 'Chris, is it?'

'Yeah. Is everyone here from Scarlett's movie?'

Joel looked affronted, and Chris felt anxious that he might be the director or something. With his Jesus Christ hair he looked quite like Eric Stoltz, although his stubby goatee ruined the whole effect.

'Yeah,' he said eventually.

'And did you all come straight from the set?'

'No,' he said, shrugging, 'not today.'

Chris could see a prolonged conversation with Joel wasn't an option, and drank his lager in silence until Scarlett clapped her hands together and said it was time to go.

'You know there's this club in Soho that does Brat Pack cocktails,' Joel told Scarlett as they walked through the crowds. 'The Lowe, the Sheedy, things like that.'

'Well, I suppose we should have gone there then,' Scarlett replied, her tone tart.

There was a queue outside the cinema. A few of the audience had dressed up, but with less enthusiasm than Scarlett's crowd. They waited until their tickets were checked. Once inside the cinema, they tried to find an empty row. Normal seating rules didn't apply at the Prince Charles, where the whole auditorium was tilted like a sinking ship and if you could see the screen you felt privileged.

'Where do you want to sit?' Chris asked Scarlett.

'I think the middle's best.'

Chris dropped back with Andy and his brother as they filed into their row. Scarlett helped Chris keep a space next to him for when Becca showed up. Andy's brother got up to get popcorn and drinks, only to be lumbered with orders from the whole group.

'You OK?' Chris asked Andy.

He nodded, taking a Lucozade bottle from his pocket and unscrewing the lid. 'What's the order of the films?'

Chris looked at the glossy flyer he'd picked up on the way in. '*Pretty in Pink, Heathers, The Breakfast Club, She's All That, Never Been Kissed, Porky's, American Pie, Ferris Bueller.*'

'*Ferris* last?'

'Yeah, why?'

'No real reason. I just haven't seen that one for a while. All the others I've seen recently.'

'You've seen *Pretty in Pink* recently?' Chris asked, ready to make fun.

'No. But I've seen it enough times to feel like I've seen it recently.'

'I know what you mean. It's etched onto your brain.'

'Exactly.'

The audience continued to file in. Chris kept looking for Becca, even though he'd believed Scarlett when she'd told him that she wouldn't be there until later. Sitting here with Andy and the others reminded him of countless evenings during his adolescence. Before discovering clubbing Chris and Andy had belonged to all sorts of youth clubs and social groups, and every time they'd joined anywhere there'd always been a girl Chris fancied who either had a boyfriend or hadn't decided whether she fancied him back. He supposed that was how he'd started his habit of being attracted to women on the outskirts of his social circles, especially as the same thing had been true throughout university as well.

These thoughts calmed Chris, and he began to believe that maybe moving on from Diana wouldn't be as difficult as he'd imagined. There was still the problem of Becca's boyfriend, but maybe the fact that he'd taken her out tonight wasn't such a bad sign. Maybe he was telling her he was sorry but their relationship was going nowhere. Maybe he was telling her he'd met someone else. Maybe that someone was Diana.

The first film started. Andy's brother spent the opening few minutes valiantly struggling up and down the row handing out popcorn and drinks before submitting to the shouts of the people behind him and sitting down. Chris drifted through the first film, not really paying that much attention apart from when James Spader was on screen. He quite liked Harry Dean Stanton's performance in the film too, and had to concede that although the plot was pretty crappy, it probably had the best performances of any Brat Pack film.

Ten minutes into *Heathers,* he noticed Becca come into the

cinema. Resisting the urge to wave, he waited for her to spot them and start making her way down the row to the empty seat beside him. He was just about to get up when Becca tripped and dropped her popcorn into his lap.

'Oh God,' she said, 'I'm so sorry.'

'That's OK,' he told her, 'I hardly ever wear these jeans.'

Becca reached down, about to brush the popcorn away, then stopped. Chris could see she was embarrassed and decided to try a joke.

'*True Romance*, right?'

'What?' she asked, touching her wig.

'Except I don't work in a comic shop and this isn't a Sonny Liston triple-bill.'

'Chiba,' Andy hissed.

'What?'

'It's Chiba, you idiot. Sonny Chiba.'

'Right,' said Chris, embarrassed. 'So who's Sonny Liston?'

'The boxer.'

'Right.' He turned back to Becca. 'Your costume's great, by the way.'

She smiled. 'The skirt is mine, but I found the pink V-neck and the white shirt in a charity shop. And the boots are my mother's. What about you?'

'Charity shop,' he nodded.

Someone hissed behind them, and Becca quickly sat down.

Towards the end of *Heathers*, Chris asked Becca if she fancied going into the bar for a quick drink. She nodded, and they got up.

'Don't be too long,' Andy warned. 'Our film's up next. And bring me back a pack of peanuts.'

'I'm not sure they have peanuts,' he told him.

'Popcorn, then.'

They walked down the row and went out into the bar. Anticipation of Becca's arrival had already made him nervous, and seeing her Molly Ringwald costume in the full light increased his anxiety. He often found himself going quiet in the company of people he found attractive, and was eager to avoid that tonight.

But she did look lovely. Her features were a little more rounded than Ringwald's and her eyes more compassionate, giving her a much less petulant expression. She had plucked, shaped eyebrows, but he couldn't remember if they'd been like that last time he saw her or if she'd done it to get into character.

'So I guess you end up with me,' she said, smiling.

'What?'

'The Breakfast Club.'

'Oh yeah, right.'

'Do you know what my favourite bit of that film is?'

'What?'

'Where they all get out their lunches and she's got sushi. I don't know why, it's not like it's an especially good joke or anything, but I really like that bit.' She sat down on one of the spare stools near the bar. 'What's your favourite bit?'

Chris blushed. 'I don't know.'

'I bet I know, it's the bit where your character looks up my character's skirt, isn't it?'

Chris looked at the floor.

'It is, isn't it? I knew it. I bet every guy who saw that film growing up likes that scene best. It's like Jamie Lee Curtis in *Trading Places*. You know they have parties where they keep that scene, you know the one I mean, on freeze-frame.'

'It's not really my favourite scene. It's just . . .'

'The first scene you think of. Yeah, yeah . . . you know it's not her in that scene?'

'No, I didn't. But it doesn't surprise me. There's that story about how she didn't do *Blue Velvet* because someone told her it was all about bugs and stuff.'

'Really?' Becca turned to the barman. 'What would you like to drink?'

'Um, beer, thanks.'

Becca ordered the drinks. 'So who else do you know who's here?'

'Just Scarlett and the people I came with. Andy, and his brother. I think it's mostly people from the film.'

'D'you know if the writer's here? I think his name's . . .'

'Joel?'

'That's right. Is he a friend of yours?'

'No, I just met him tonight. In the bar before we came over. He seemed a bit weird.'

Becca laughed. 'I'm glad you think that. I met him at Scarlett's party . . . you weren't at that, right?'

'No, I was, I arrived late.'

'Oh, OK, right, well, anyway, he made me go upstairs with him into Becca's study and answer questions.'

'What sort of questions?' asked Chris, shocked.

'You know, stupid movie questions. Trivia questions. What year did *Porky's* come out and stuff like that.'

'They're showing that tonight.'

'*Porky's*?' She looked away. 'Do you want to get your friend's popcorn? We should probably go back in a minute.'

'Do you want anything else?'

'No, I'm fine.'

Chris went to get Andy's popcorn. He felt pleased about his conversation with Becca, although he wished it hadn't been so brief and he'd done more of the talking. Still, she seemed friendly, and less reserved than she'd been during their first meeting.

The credits to *Heathers* were still rolling as they went back in. Andy thanked Chris as he handed him his popcorn.

The ColourMePink offices were in Battersea. This surprised Becca, who'd assumed that all major production companies were in Soho. It also made her wonder once again about the quality of this production, and whether it was something she wanted to be involved with. James' argument that it was better to be working on something no matter what it was had never convinced her, and she only really wanted to be involved with the programme if it was likely to be a success. She was also slightly troubled by everything Diana had told her about the complex structure of the series. It sounded like they might want to tie people up indefinitely, and she wanted to be able to get out of it if it didn't turn out to be a pleasant experience.

She arrived early, which proved prudent, as even with precise instructions the offices were impossible to find. With no real sign or number outside, the only indication that she'd reached the right place was a door that'd been painted with pink gloss paint. Becca pressed a button on the intercom alongside the door and waited to be buzzed in. She walked up the two flights of stairs and then into a large waiting area that reminded her of the reception scene from *The King of Comedy*. Going up to the surprisingly elderly woman behind the desk, she told her that she was there to see Brian. The receptionist told her to wait and rang one of the other rooms. She talked for a moment, then looked back up at Becca.

'If you'd like to take a seat, love, he'll be ready for you in a minute.'

Becca walked over to the distressed leather sofa. It was hard to tell if it was a genuinely old sofa, or had been designed to look that way. Either way, it was comfortable, and after getting herself a cup of water and picking up one of the issues of *Variety* that were fanned out on the reception table, she didn't mind waiting. She enjoyed the adverts for films in production, and catching up on who'd been cast in projects she'd read about. It was almost disappointing when Brian appeared.

'Becca, right?' he asked, as he walked over to her.

'Yeah,' she said, standing up. 'Are you Brian?'

'I certainly am,' he replied, smiling. 'Shall we go through to my office?'

'OK.'

'Actually, no, let's go into the conference room. It's much more comfortable in there. Can I get you anything to drink?'

'No, I'm fine with water.'

'You sure?' He looked at her, and then started walking towards the conference room. He was wearing a black short-sleeved shirt with a pair of expensive jeans and trainers. He was slightly shorter than Becca, and his black hair was thinning on top. The conference room was painted white, with a TV and video set up in the corner. On a whiteboard along the right wall someone had drawn out a complex tree-diagram which seemed to refer to events in Diana's TV series.

'OK,' he said, 'I thought it'd be best if we just had an informal chat. You come highly recommended, and Diana clearly rates you, so let me tell you a little bit about the programme, and then if you've got any questions you want to ask me, fire away.'

Becca listened to Brian as he repeated the same hype she'd already heard twice from Diana. Whoever this incredible scriptwriter was, he'd done an amazing job of persuading these people of his genius. Neither Brian nor Diana seemed that interested in the director, apart from the fact that he had a film background. Becca was surprised at this reverence. Although she hadn't worked on many drama programmes before, she knew enough about them to understand that it was rare for one writer to be singled out for praise, especially someone so young.

'So this guy is writing the whole series himself?'

Brian smiled. 'It's unusual, isn't it? We did have a team all set up, and we were fairly certain that that was the way we were going to go, but then we looked at a couple of scripts and spoke to his agent and decided to let him have a crack at the whole series. We started off with the usual standard sort of agreement that he would write fifty per cent of the series, but then when we looked at the first couple of episodes, they were so good, and so immaculately conceived that it seemed ridiculous to take the rest of the scripts away from him. Don't tell anyone else I told you this, but he does have a tiny problem doing the final polish . . . he's very temperamental, the complete opposite of most scriptwriters, who are so fucking desperate to get something on TV that they'll do any fucking thing you tell them . . . so we have a couple of people who go over the fine details, and then our director is keen to let the actors improvise a bit as well, but the essential conception of the whole thing is his alone.'

'That's unusual . . .'

'It is, isn't it? To be honest, I think this'll be his only real big project, unless he finds something else that he can psychologically relate to in the same way. I don't think this project is autobiographical . . . it's all about women for a start, but there's something personal about it for him. It's probably a really good job that it's got all this spin-off potential, and that it's got the sort of soap element so it can go on for ages. I'll tell you who this guy's most like . . . you know that guy Joss Whedon who does *Buffy the Vampire Slayer* and he had that one idea and first of all he tried it as a movie. You remember that, with Kristy Swanson?'

He looked at Becca. She nodded, worried they were about to get into film tag.

'Well, that was a flop, so he tried it again as a TV series and now it's a hit and there's all these imitations and spin-offs. That's what it's going to be like with *Kiss*.'

'You think it'll be as big as *Buffy*?' she asked, wanting to hear some hyperbole.

'It's not the same sort of thing, and this is twentysomethings instead of high school. And there's nothing supernatural about it . . . and it's English, of course . . . but I see no reason why it can't be as big as something like *Melrose Place*. We've got the same slot lined up on Channel Five.'

Becca drifted out as he started talking about the show again. She wasn't sure why she'd come here today, especially as she'd felt certain from the beginning that she was going to turn down the job. She supposed she was doing it for James, so she could say that at least she tried, but that was an excuse. She'd come here because she'd hoped to find out more about Diana, and through her, Chris.

'So, is there anything you'd like to ask me?' Brian eventually asked her.

'Actually,' Becca said, looking at her watch, 'I want to apologise.'

'What for?'

'I'm sorry, I shouldn't have come in for this interview. I really don't feel I'm up to the job.'

'Why? I'm sure you'd be great.'

'It's nice of you to say so, but I just don't think I'm equipped to work on this show. It's obviously going to be a big success, and I hate turning down an opportunity like this, and I know I'll be kicking myself when I see the rest of you winning awards, but I don't really have the background. If I'd done more work in drama, I'd feel happier, but I'm worried I'll let you down.'

Brian took a long, appraising look at her. Realising it wasn't a bluff, he said,

'I'm sorry to hear that, but I do understand. The only thing is, Diana had led me to believe you'd definitely want the job. It's fine that you don't, but it means I've got to find someone quickly. It's never a problem to get someone at short notice but I need a person I can totally rely on. I don't suppose you know anyone who could handle it?'

Becca got out her address book and spent the next ten minutes helping Brian with potential candidates for the job. She'd warmed to him in the course of the interview, and slightly regretted now not taking it further. But she knew it'd make more sense not to, and she was relieved that she wouldn't be working with Diana. She thanked Brian for his time, left the office, and after spending ten minutes trying to get back to the tube, finally found the right road and caught the train home.

'Why won't you give me her number?'

'Because she's already asked for yours. I'm helping you play it cool. Besides, what are you going to do if James picks up?'

'Sell him double-glazing. Look, I have been in this situation before.'

'Relax, Chris, it'll be so much easier if you let Auntie Scarlett sort things out. I know what you're going through, but this isn't a normal who-phones-who situation. It's not like she's sitting at home thinking you're not interested . . . she has to be gently wooed away.'

'How can I woo if I can't talk to her?'

'Relationships don't develop when lovers are together, it's the time apart that counts.'

Chris considered this. Feeling slightly calmer, he said, 'So when did she ask for my number?'

'Yesterday afternoon.' Scarlett swallowed. 'My guess is she'll call today.'

Chris had experienced several serious mood swings over the weekend. Becca had left three films before the end of Twelve Hour Teens, giving him a goodnight kiss that was just a little too passionate to count as merely friendly. Chris was usually desperate for bed after staying up all night, but breakfast with Scarlett and her friends kept him awake a few hours longer.

Sleeping through Saturday left him feeling foul, and when he woke up at midnight he got so depressed that he foolishly took a tube into Soho and went to an after-hours actors' bar that Diana had got him into. The place was packed with friends of hers, and he soon decided to leave. But as he got up to go, his path was blocked by Annabel.

'Chris,' she cried, throwing her arms around him, 'how are you?'

'OK.'

She released him from her embrace and gently pushed him back. 'So who are you here with?'

'Oh, no one, actually. I went to this film marathon thing with Scarlett and her friends last night and it carried on until this morning so I've only just got up. I was hoping some of them might be here.'

'I don't think Scarlett's a member, is she?'

'Isn't she? Oh well. I just got up too late to organise a proper night out, but I felt depressed staying in on my own.'

Annabel nodded. 'I understand. But you've run into me now, so everything's OK. Why don't you come and have a drink with me and Mark?'

'Who's Mark?'

'My new boyfriend. Didn't Diana mention him?'

'Did she meet him when she was staying at yours?'

'That's right. Come on over and I'll introduce you.'

Mark turned out to be a surprisingly decent guy. His good humour had clearly mellowed Annabel, and after three more rounds Chris forgot he was drinking with a former enemy and started enjoying himself. He'd always tried to get on with Annabel, aware that it was unwise to alienate his girlfriend's best friend, but they'd fallen out badly a few months after Chris and Diana had properly got together.

It'd taken him a while to spot the problem. When he'd first met Diana she was sharing a flat with Annabel and he'd delighted in spending time there. The two women had developed an extremely close friendship, but he didn't feel excluded as their private language was mainly lines from their favourite films. As his taste wasn't that different, he thought he was slowly becoming the privileged third member of their gang. But Annabel soon became offhand with him, and he realised she felt jealous of their relationship. The fatal rift had come one night when he'd jokingly said to her,

'You know, Annabel, I've got no interest in shutting you out. Diana belongs to you as much as she belongs to me.'

Her reply had been brilliant.

'Diana doesn't belong to anyone.'

After that they became openly hostile, only backing off when occasion demanded. Chris pressed Diana to leave Annabel's flat, and eventually she gave in and they got a place together. Since then, Chris and Annabel had barely spoken, but now that he'd broken up with Diana, Annabel seemed to want to be friends again. He knew it was suspicious, but somehow even if Annabel did have an evil plan, it'd seemed preferable to stay here and find out what it was than go back to his empty flat. Besides, his body-clock had been put completely out of kilter by the previous night, and he knew he wouldn't be able to get to sleep for hours. As it drew near to the club's closing time, Annabel said,

'Would you like to come back for a bit more of a chat?'

There was absolutely no reason for him to take her up on her offer, but five minutes later they were in a taxi and away in the opposite direction to her flat. It didn't seem a really stupid idea until after the first few glasses of whisky, when Chris was in tears, Mark was embarrassed and Annabel was doling out patronising advice. He hated himself for opening up in what was so clearly the wrong company, and left their flat without even thinking how he was going to get home.

Not wanting to call Andy's brother, he got a night bus and walked the rest of the way. Memories of this episode distressed him for most of Sunday and Monday and made him vow to stay at home next time he woke up at midnight. By Tuesday, he'd decided the only thing that could possibly salvage his week was talking to Becca, and after talking to Scarlett, he remained miserable until three o'clock, when the phone rang.

'Hello?'

'Hi, is that Chris?'

'Yeah.'

'It's Becca.'

'Oh,' he said, smiling, 'thanks for calling.'

'I hope it's OK. I got your number from Scarlett.'

'No, it's fine. I mean, it's great.'

'Good. Look, the reason I'm calling is that I really enjoyed Friday night. It was great to see you again.' She hesitated. 'And your funny friend and his brother.'

Chris carried the phone into the lounge. 'It was great to see you too.'

'Good. I was just a bit worried in case . . . well, it had been a weird evening for me, before I got to the cinema, I mean. That was why I was so . . . I don't know . . . giddy or whatever when I arrived. I'm sorry if I embarrassed you.'

'Scarlett said.'

'Said what?'

'That things were difficult for you.'

'Really?'

'Yeah, she said you'd gone out with your boyfriend or something . . .'

'Oh . . .' she replied. 'So you know that?'

'Yeah.'

Becca was quiet for a moment. 'Is that a problem?'

'I don't know. I mean, it depends. Is it a problem for you?'

'I don't know. I've never done this before.'

'Done what?'

She laughed. 'Right.'

'So, are we going to get to know each other better?'

She giggled.

'What?' he asked, defensive.

'I'm sorry, it's just the way you said that.'

'Sleazy, right?'

'Not sleazy. Just a bit . . . Woody Allen.'

'Before or after Soon-Yi?'

She laughed. 'Oh no, prime period Woody. When all that schtick was still appealing.'

'Thanks, I think. So how do you want me to put it?'

'I don't want you to put it. Look, Chris, I'm going to be frank with you. I'm not looking for an affair.'

'Right. So what do you want?'

'I don't know. I just, like I said, really enjoyed being in the cinema with you.'

'So that's what you want to do, is it? Go to the cinema together?'

'Yeah, but it's not just that. I thought, first, if you wanted, we could go for lunch.'

'Is that allowed?'

'I don't see why not.'

'OK,' he said, 'where do you want to go?'

'I don't know. Somewhere near you.'

'OK. Do you want to come to my place?'

'That'd be great.'

'When?'

'How about tomorrow?'

'OK. What time?'

'Twelve.'

'Twelve, great.'

'Great.'

He replaced the receiver. Then, panicking, he picked up the phone and dialled 1471, worrying she would have withheld her number. But no, there it was.

'Becca?' he said, once he'd been connected.

'Yes?'

'Don't you want to know where I live?'

Becca was furious with herself. Fortunately, Chris had only thought she was absent-minded, but that slip could've given the whole game away. And just because he didn't realise now didn't mean he wouldn't think back to the call and work out what was going on at some point in the future.

She looked at the clock, still unsure whether this whole thing was a mistake. At the moment, everything was working out in her favour, and even James was being nice to her, which she put down to him subconsciously sensing that he had a rival for her affections. But no doubt this period wouldn't last, and by encouraging Chris she was asking for trouble.

The thing that worried her most about Chris was that he reminded her of men from her past. OK, in all the important ways he was different. He didn't seem vain, or sullen or excessively weird. And if his interest in films was unusually passionate, at least that was an obsession she shared. There was also something about him that appealed to the younger side of her. She knew if she left James and moved in with Chris she'd be much less worried about finding a job, but she also knew that all her bad habits would soon resurface. It wouldn't be long before she was back to staying up all night, sleeping during the day and watching films every night of the week. And while she already knew how much she loved this lifestyle, it felt like a step backwards, as disappointing as picking up an addiction she'd previously conquered.

Still, if she played it right, maybe she'd be able to stay with James and still have Chris in her life. The first set-up scene had been spoilt by the unexpected appearance of Scarlett, but since then everything had worked like a dream.

Like a film.

Chris hated this bit. He knew there were people out there who lived for these moments, who called it romance and read books and watched films for precisely these periods of anticipation; people who wore out their copies of *Grease* by repeatedly rewinding to the bit where Sandra Dee is floating Rizzo's thin sheets of scented paper on pondwater while singing and thinking of Danny Zuko's face, but for him it was just annoying.

Especially as he still had no idea whether this was going to turn into something. In spite of her protests, he felt sure she did want an affair. He'd just have to go slowly, that was all. And that was fine.

He got dressed and walked back into the lounge, trying to decide whether to attempt some work on his book. He wasn't really in the mood, but he supposed the best thing to do would be to write a chapter about moments like this in romantic films. He already had one example, *Grease*, and it wouldn't take him long to come up with others. After all, nearly all romantic movies had a stage between the lovers meeting and them going to bed. It was a stage that was becoming less frequently represented in films, however, and modern screenwriters had to come up with increasingly complicated ways to stop couples mating on their first meeting.

He turned his chair to face the desk, and took his pad from the drawer. Then he went out into the kitchen to pour himself a large glass of orange juice. He took the ice-tray from the chill-cabinet and snapped three cubes into the glass. Then he took a packet of Jaffa Cakes from the top cupboard and carried everything back into the front room.

He sat back at the desk, still feeling restless. He looked at his TV and video, trying to decide whether he needed to watch something to get himself going. Since he'd really started to get to grips with this study, he'd realised that focusing on romantic comedies was a surprisingly smart move. They seemed somehow much denser than most mainstream movies. He knew lots of modern film theorists liked to focus on action films or event movies, keen to apply their abstract ideas to the most commercial of Hollywood projects, but Chris found those sorts of films and that sort of theory soulless.

He was so relieved that Becca had admitted she had a boyfriend. It had been obvious from the first time he met her that she wasn't a single woman. Not just because she was attractive, but because she seemed unfulfilled rather than lonely. And the fact that she'd come clean about it made him feel much less nervous. He wasn't the sort of man who usually had affairs with women who were already in relationships, but he had done so before, and there'd been more than one occasion in the past when there'd been cross-over periods between his relationships.

Most of his friends were much more moralistic about stuff like that, at least until they got caught out. Chris wasn't exactly the playboy type, and had little time for the emotional arrangement necessary to maintain open relationships, but he also believed that concern about convention often came in the way of happiness. Deep down, he believed that when something pleasurable happened to you, it was silly to feel scared about it.

He closed his eyes and tried to picture Becca. In some ways, this was always the sweetest part of a relationship, and Chris hoped he would dream of his mysterious stranger tonight.

Because after tomorrow, he realised, everything would be different.

Becca left her flat and walked to the tube. When she reached Chris's place she pressed his buzzer and waited for him to come downstairs. He was smart but inadequately dressed for the weather, which impressed Becca, as it indicated that he was more concerned with looking good for lunch than his own comfort.

'I've found a decent place for us to eat,' he told her. 'At least, I think it'll be alright. I haven't been here that long.'

He locked the front door and walked over to her. Becca couldn't help feeling that she should be locking the door and coming over to him. She wondered if she'd ever shake the feeling he was living in her home. As they started walking she realised he wasn't going to tell her the name of the restaurant.

'So where are we going?'

'Oh,' he said, 'it's just a small Italian place.'

She laughed. 'I knew it.'

'What?' he asked, lips concerned.

'Nothing,' she said. 'It's just that I know this area quite well.'

'And?'

'And when I asked you to choose where we were going to go for lunch I had a little bet with myself about where you'd pick.'

'So it was a test?'

He looked at her and she felt guilty, then tried to apologise by taking his arm. He seemed uncomfortable with this gesture, first patting her fingers and then holding his arm too stiffly.

'Well, yes, but it was a nice test. It's not as if I'd have thought bad of you if you'd chosen somewhere else.'

He didn't say anything. Becca could tell he felt tense with her, and pulled his arm to make him stop walking.

'Tell me what's wrong.'

He bit his lip. 'I don't know. I feel awkward.'

'Why?'

'I don't know what the rules are.'

Becca looked at her feet. 'There aren't any rules. Look, you remember last night when we were talking about Woody Allen?'

'Of course.'

'Well, would it make things easier for you if we did the *Annie Hall* thing?'

He looked at her. 'Do you mean the kissing thing?'

She smiled. 'I knew you'd know what I meant. Go on then. Unless you don't want to.'

'No, of course I want to. But you haven't changed your mind about us just being friends?'

She shook her head. 'I'm sorry, Chris, I'm just not looking for that right now.'

'So it'd be a friendly kiss?'

Becca brushed her fringe out of her eyes. 'I'm not saying we should deny feeling attracted to each other. I wouldn't be here with you if you weren't someone I could go out with.'

'OK,' he said, 'I guess my ego can cope with that.'

'Great,' she said, and kissed him.

The restaurant was busier than Becca remembered it ever being and she was glad to be surrounded by people: it made the next planned scene so much easier. It was quite a sleazy choice, but she'd been scared off going for anything mainstream after seeing his video collection. She wanted him to pick up what she was doing eventually, but for the moment she wanted him to understand it only in a vague way, tiny echoes and hints that would trouble him when he was alone.

'It's not really a Woody Allen situation though, is it?'

'No?' she asked, opening the menu.

'No, we're not really Woody Allen characters. At least I know I'm not.'

'You could be. Maybe in one of those films that he's not in. I could see you as a John Cusack.'

'Oh, God, don't.'

'What? Don't you like John Cusack?'

He grinned. 'I used to love John Cusack. As a kid I wanted to be John Cusack. But then I found out that in real life he doesn't have to do all that nervous stuff with women. I really hate it when there's an actor who always play characters who have to be charming and pull off all these elaborate scams to get the girl, and then you find out in real life they're a successful Lothario. I think I really went off John Cusack when I heard about him and Minnie Driver. Oh, and I hate *Grosse Pointe Blank*. I think it's one of the worst films I've ever seen.'

Becca relaxed in her chair. The chairs in this restaurant were ill-matched with the table. They were fine for reclining in, but when the food arrived the only way to eat successfully was to perch on the edge of the seat-cushion.

'But he's been in some good stuff since then.'

'I know,' he said. 'I'm being unfair. It's always weird with the actors you like when you're young. You kid yourself that there's no difference between them and you, and then it's always a shock when you find out what they're really like.'

A waiter appeared. They ordered, and Chris got up to use the toilet. While he was gone, the waiter brought across a bottle of white wine and two glasses. Becca played with the stem of hers, twirling the bottom of the glass across the table. Chris returned.

'Is this a *When Harry Met Sally* thing?'

She looked up. 'What d'you mean?'

'You know, can men and women ever be friends, or does sex always get in the way?'

'Would you like it to be a *When Harry Met Sally* thing?'

He looked at her. 'Can I tell you something embarrassing?'

'Of course.'

'I've seen that film twelve times.'

She laughed. 'Why's that embarrassing?'

'I don't know. Men aren't supposed to be able to like romances like that. They even put that in the films themselves. Look at all that stuff about girl films and guy films in *Sleepless in Seattle*.'

'Is that in *Sleepless in Seattle*?'

'I think so, isn't it? Is the bit about *The Godfather* in that film or *You've Got Mail*?'

'*You've Got Mail*, I think. Maybe I've got that wrong. Anyway, explain more about why you were embarrassed to tell me how many times you've seen *When Harry Met Sally*.'

'OK,' he said, looking at her. 'Because it was one of those films that fitted perfectly with a particular stage in my life. When I watched that film it was almost as if I wasn't seeing the characters up on screen but myself and somebody else.'

'You don't seem the Billy Crystal type.'

'I'm not,' he said, quickly, 'and of course that doesn't really make sense. I mean, my Sally wasn't someone I'd known for years and years and we didn't have all that time together and then get married or anything like that . . .'

'But?'

'But I knew how they felt. I knew how it was to have a special person. And how sometimes it can be even better to have a special person . . .'

Becca giggled, then put a hand over her mouth. 'I'm sorry,

Chris, I'm not mocking the sentiment. It's just the words, special person, they sound like . . .'

'Special purpose, right?'

She laughed. 'I knew you'd get it. I bet you like Steve Martin more than Woody Allen, don't you?'

'The early stuff.'

'Of course, that's what I meant. But I'm sorry to have interrupted. Carry on with what you were saying. Sometimes it can be even better to have a special person . . .'

'Who's not your girlfriend, because then you get to spin out the getting-to-know-them stage . . .'

'Which is always the best part of any relationship.'

'Exactly. It's so . . . *heady*.'

'No pun intended.'

'Oh, come on, I'm being serious.'

Becca sipped her wine. 'Do you mean all this?'

'Of course.' He looked at her. 'Why?'

'It just seems an abrupt change. A minute ago you felt awkward about this, and now you seem to have exactly the same thoughts as me.'

'That's because I feel comfortable with you now.'

'Why? Because of the kiss?'

'Because you've explained the rules. Oh, and the kiss as well, I suppose.'

She smiled. 'Were you afraid of me before?'

'A little bit,' he admitted. 'You did come into my life quite abruptly.'

'And that scared you?'

'Not scared, exactly. I just felt something. Love affairs always start on a strange level for me.'

'What d'you mean, a strange level?'

The waiter slid Becca's starter in front of her. She ignored him, holding Chris's gaze. Chris's abstract comment had chimed with something inside her, and she was eager for him to explain further. But instead he looked away, smiling as the waiter placed his food in front of him. Becca was still waiting for the right moment to start her scene, distracted by their surprisingly compatible conversation.

'Sorry,' he said, tasting his food, 'I don't really know what I'm talking about.'

'No, don't say that. Explain it to me. It doesn't matter if it sounds pretentious. I'm really interested.'

'It's not a startlingly original observation,' he told her. 'All I mean is that every time I've had a relationship that's turned out to be really worthwhile, there's been a sort of magic moment . . . some little cosmic kink. I'm sorry, this is such wank.'

'No,' she said, 'it isn't. Go on, tell me more.'

He looked away. 'Every time I've fallen in love, it's been with someone on the edge of my social circle. It's got so I can spot who I'm going to end up with from the moment I meet them. And with you I had that feeling, but I thought that this time it was going to be different. I thought you were a complete stranger. And then I find out that you *are* on the edge of my social circle.'

'No, no, no,' said Becca, shaking her head, 'that wasn't what you were talking about. Don't back off. I really want to hear this.'

Chris didn't say anything, and carried on eating his lunch. Becca felt an urge to pick up his plate and hurl it onto the floor, but she didn't want to scare him. She couldn't tell if he was deliberately teasing her, or if he was embarrassed, or what. Many of her previous peculiar partners had wooed her with strange theories about love or romance, and she was getting a strong feeling of *déjà vu* from the stuff he'd been saying. But he no longer seemed willing to humour her.

'Tell me about your boyfriend.'

'What?' she said, startled.

'It's only fair. I should know what I'm up against.'

'What d'you mean, up against? I thought you said you understood.'

'I do. But I want to know about the man you love.'

'I don't really want to talk about him.'

'Why not?'

'It makes me feel uncomfortable. I'll tell you another time, OK?' She pushed her plate away. 'Let's play a game instead.'

'Truth or dare?'

'No,' she said, 'not truth or dare. A different game. Pick a couple, and then tell me their story.'

'Oh, God, do we have to?'

'Yes,' she said.

'Then will you tell me about your boyfriend?'

'No,' she said, 'I'll tell you about him when we know each other better.'

'Can we play truth or dare then too?'

'If you're good. Now pick a couple.'

Becca's Dodgy Boyfriends #4
Jason

Jason came along soon after Colin. After three nutters, he initially seemed comparatively normal. Even her mother, who had hated everyone else she'd brought home, had to admit that he had a certain sulky charm. Six foot three, long-haired, never to be seen in anything other than his jeans and a T-shirt, he only became a liability after he chucked Becca and then decided he wanted her back.

It was completely out of character for her not to accept his excuses, but at the time her career had been going particularly well and she was enjoying the company of her friends too much to devote all her time to an emotional ex. When it finally sunk in that she wasn't going to take him back, he started sending her tapes full of songs that they'd listened to when they were together.

He did, eventually, get over her, and for a while they were friends again, going out to restaurants and studiously avoiding the subject of their relationship. A year ago, she'd received an invitation to his wedding, but hadn't been able to bring herself to attend.

The first time his mother went to America, Chris was thirteen. She was petrified about the trip, and even made a will before she left. At that age, Chris's life was pretty much entirely books and records. When she asked him what he wanted for a present, he told her to buy him an American book that wasn't available in England. Preferably something to do with movies.

She brought him back a catalogue from a New York video shop.

Chris's mum was hopeless about movies, but brilliant at helping him with his private life. One time she'd guessed he'd swapped girlfriends just by catching him reading a different horoscope in a magazine, and Chris knew she'd be the perfect person to talk to about Becca.

He found his clock and checked the time. Five-thirty. It'd take about an hour to get over to his mother's, so he didn't have too much time to fill. He picked up his remote and ejected Diana's rehearsal tape. It had hardly been out of his recorder since he'd moved in, and although he did watch other videos, he kept this cassette on top of the machine and most days watched at least a few minutes of her reading from various plays. Chris knew this wasn't healthy, but tried not to think about it, telling himself that in a few days he'd toss the tape away for good.

He slid the tape from the slot and returned it to a pile alongside the television. He looked round at the clutter that had begun to build up and wondered whether he should have a quick tidy. It occurred to him that he'd been the only person to see the inside of his flat since Andy and his brother had moved him in. Oh, and that woman who'd come over to drop off the key to the French windows. His mysterious landlady, a woman he'd like to meet. It probably wasn't all that amazing that she liked *Drugstore Cowboy*, but that hadn't stopped him imagining a completely compatible unknown partner.

Chris wondered if he should invite someone over. Maybe he needed that kind of prompt to feel it was worth tidying up. He'd never really been the kind of person to socialise inside his house, preferring not to spend too much time indoors. Unless he was working on something or watching a video, Chris accepted any excuse to go out, and any real domestication of the space he inhabited had always been made by his previous partners. Diana was especially good at that, and their last place had ended up looking extremely inviting by the time they came to move out. But even then they hardly ever had anyone over if they could avoid it, and aside from the occasional evening with Andy, no one really visited. Chris thought that whether people enjoyed being in someone's house had less to do with the state of the house than what the person was like. Certain people seemed to welcome others into their space. Chris had never really been like that.

But maybe he could make more effort. He wanted Becca to come here, after all, and no doubt she'd prove more willing if he could convey to her that being inside his flat was a pleasant experience. It certainly felt like a nice space, and he sensed human warmth stored within these walls.

He picked up a plate from the coffee table and carried it through to the kitchen, still thinking about Becca. He knew he should be more honest with himself, and wondered why he felt so squeamish about self-analysis. The truth was, he did know why it'd excited Becca when he told her that love affairs started on a strange level for him. She was taken with his comment because it let her know that he was complicit in the romance she was constructing. Becca was looking for something, he could tell, and he believed that she had yet to decide whether the something was him, or the situation. If it was just the situation, there would be no progression in their relationship. Things would continue, grow increasingly tense, and then one day it would stop, and depending on how things had gone, they'd either become lifelong friends, or if that was too difficult, gradually forget about each other.

Chris usually took a cynical attitude towards the start of relationships. While most of the women he'd gone out with had, on the whole, turned out to be decent people, he'd yet to find himself excited by anyone who wasn't slightly strange, and the early part of most of his previous relationships had been devoted to working out whether the woman he fancied was too weird to date. And once he'd decided that, he also had to discover whether they would accommodate his own oddities. Only after that was settled could he consider getting serious with someone.

He suspected Becca felt much the same way. She shared his whimsical nature, which probably made her as much of a freak-magnet as he was. And no doubt she was just as determined to find someone she could stay with for ever. Chris knew finding a lifelong partner would be extremely difficult, and might never happen at all if he started out with that aim. Far better to continue muddling along and hope he lucked into a relationship strong enough to last beyond the usual couple of years of compatibility.

Most of the couples Chris had known had only run into trouble when they contemplated the possibility of permanence, a consideration bound to upset a relationship's equilibrium. Sometimes it struck him as strange that while he didn't know any couples who had broken up because of infidelity or drug problems or any other present-tense misdeeds, he knew loads who'd split over babies, or because one partner couldn't imagine spending the rest of their life with the other, or simply because the reality of the relationship had become too pressing. It was almost as if his entire generation had decided to be nice to each other and they discovered they weren't up to the task.

'I made some spaghetti,' Chris's mum told him, as he arrived at her house and they walked through to the kitchen. 'I've already eaten mine, but it's there if you want it.'

'Maybe in a little while. Do you have anything to drink?'

'Alcohol? I could open a bottle of wine. Or I think there may be some beer in the fridge.'

'Beer would be great. Don't worry, I'll get it.'

He went to the kitchen, opened the fridge and took out a bottle. He found an opener in the drawer beneath the sink, uncapped it and came back into the living room.

'So what's wrong?' she asked. 'You sounded strange on the phone.'

Chris looked at his mum, and then told her everything.

Chris's Favourite Films #9
Repo Man

Many of the films on Chris's list took a while to get there. Unlike Andy, he believed that for a film to be truly great, you had to be able to watch it at least five times. This was why, for example, he thought that *The Shining* was better than *Dr Strangelove*, even though he could accept that most people probably thought the latter was the better film. Sometimes this fitted with conventional opinion (Chris believed that the reason why *Vertigo* was most people's favourite Hitchcock film was because you could watch it over and over again). Other times, it was another contributing factor to why people thought his opinions were so perverse.

For a long time, Chris was fond of *Repo Man* mainly because he could never remember what happened in it. He couldn't remember the plot, the characters, even a particularly memorable scene. After watching it twice on the same weekend, however, it began to stick in his mind. Now he liked it mainly for Emilio Estevez's performance, especially the bit where he responds to an emotional blow by singing a song about his favourite TV shows. Often when things were going badly for Chris, he'd find himself running through these lyrics, and knowing that even if TV wasn't going to make him happy, no doubt a movie would soon appear that might do the trick.

Becca noticed Chris waiting for her outside the television repair shop where they had arranged to meet. She walked up to him and kissed him softly on the lips. He smiled. She brought a small paper diamond from behind her back.

'What's that?' he asked. 'Today's activity?'

'Yes,' she replied.

'Origami?'

'No, this is how we decide what we're doing. Pick a colour. You remember . . . didn't you ever do this in school?'

'OK, blue.'

'B . . . L . . . U . . . E,' she said, folding the corners in and out and again. 'Now pick a number.'

'Six.'

'1 . . . 2 . . . 3 . . . 4 . . . 5 . . . 6,' she counted, stopping and waiting for Chris to point to another number.

'Three.'

She counted this out, and then asked him again. He pointed, and she unfolded the paper flap, looking at what was written beneath and nodding. 'OK, yes, good. Right, we need a bus.'

'Where are we going?'

'I can't tell you. That'd spoil the surprise.'

'Well, which bus do we need?'

'The 107,' she told him, pointing up the street. 'Come on.'

They didn't have long to wait for a bus. Becca stood back and let Chris get on first, then followed him down the aisle to the back seat. She leaned against the window, squashing the side of her face against the glass.

'I had a dream about you last night,' she told him, 'but I'm embarrassed to tell you what happened.'

Chris blushed. 'Don't be embarrassed, I've had lots of dreams about you.'

'Really?' she said, looking at him. 'Let's swap. Tell me your favourite dream about me.'

'It's stupid. I'm living in France, I don't know why, and you're a famous actress. There's a big poster of you for this film you're in . . . it's a blue poster, but not like *Three Colours Blue* or anything like that, it's more moody and glamorous, like a perfume advert or something . . .'

'That's not a dream about me. That's about your ex-girlfriend.'

'What d'you mean?'

'She's the actress, not me.'

'How d'you know that?'

'You told me.'

'Did I? I don't remember. But the dream is about you, really. The part about you being an actress isn't the important bit. That's just an aside, and you're right, that might have been influenced by Diana.'

'OK, I forgive you, go on . . .'

He leaned back. 'Right, and I'm on my own . . . I'm pretty sure it's in Paris, although I've only been there once in real life . . . and somehow I end up winning a free ticket to this really glamorous gala performance, and when I get there I discover that I'm sitting in the front row next to you. At first you're really pissed off because you're a big star and I'm a nobody, but after a while you start talking to me . . . I'm talking in English and you're taking in French, although we can understand each other perfectly.'

138

Becca nodded. 'I like the part about me being a big star.'

'And we talk, and you ask me what I do, and I don't really answer . . . I just mumble and tell you that I do odd bits of writing, essays and stuff, and you tell me there's a word in French for people like that, and you say this excellent word, it's more of a phrase, but I can't remember what it is. And in the dream, I'm all unshaven and my hair's a bit dishevelled and I've got a neat close-fitting Brad Pitt-style leather jacket, and then you begin to notice me a bit more, but before anything can happen the curtains open and the film begins.'

The bus rolled over a bump. Chris put his hand on the seat in front.

'The rest of the dream was just us two sitting watching the film together, feeling really attracted, but unable to do anything because we're in a cinema. That bit's based on real life too. Back when I was a film reviewer I had to review *The Hairdresser's Husband*, and no one else showed up for the press screening so I ended up sitting with one of the women who worked in the cinema, and there was this real tension that was awkward because we were watching this erotic movie.'

'Do you want me to tell you about my dream now?'

'It's only fair.'

'OK, but I have to warn you that it's quite a weird one. Basically, it's a recurring dream I've had ever since I was a child, but this time you were in it and I think your presence may have brought the dream to a resolution.' She stopped, using a gloved finger to wipe a loose strand of hair from her lipsticked mouth. 'I think the dream comes from spending so many of my teenage years in the cinema. Hang on, this is our stop.'

She tapped Chris's hand and he pressed the bell. He had to get up first and the two of them walked down to the middle doors and jumped down onto the pavement.

'You have to lead,' he told her, 'I've got no idea where we're going.'

'OK,' she replied. 'Don't worry, I'm just getting my bearings. I didn't think you'd choose this one.'

Chris frowned. 'This isn't something freaky, is it? I'm not a big fan of doing dares or bungee-jumping or anything like that.'

'Relax, this is a nice surprise. If I told you what we're going to do you'd be pleased, but I'm not going to because that'll spoil it.' She squinted at a street name. 'Right, I know where I'm going now. Anyway, this dream. What usually happens is that I find myself in a really big cinema ... one of those kind that they don't really have so much in England any more, not since the invasion of the multiplexes. And I'm dead. Everybody in the audience is dead. On the screen are a lot of abstract images, shot really close up, but slowly, as I watch, I realise this isn't just some obscure art movie but that it does have some sort of plot. I can't really work out exactly what's going on in the story, but there seems to be only one camera that's only showing the main character's point of view. So I ask the person next to me what's going on, and she explains that this place, this cinema, is purgatory, and what we're watching on the screen is the whole of someone's life. And we have to stay here until we've seen the whole lives of everyone who's in the cinema replayed on the screen.'

Chris was still slightly behind Becca, and she kept looking back to check his reaction.

'And these films, they're the whole of someone's lives seen through their eyes. Everything they saw in their whole lives ...'

'Including their dreams?'

'Um ... no, I don't think so. I think when the person's sleeping you just see blackness.'

'That's stupid.'

'No, it's not. Besides, it's my dream, what I say goes. And anyway, my life comes up on screen, and lots of it is films, which the audience quite likes, 'cause at least you get a bit of a story, and maybe a film you haven't seen. A lot of the dream is supposed to be about why we're all individuals, and that in this limbo state, watching these people's lives as movies, you understand the point of being isolated, and the collective experience.'

'This sounds like a very metaphysical dream.'

'So, it's metaphysical.' She laughed. 'Fuck you. Anyway, the audience sits through my life, and then the next thing that comes up is your life, and the audience is really pissed off and bored, 'cause loads of it's the same, especially after the point where we get together, all the same experiences, but also the same movies, and I start thinking it's really stupid to show couple's lives straight after each other, and then I wonder where you are. And for a moment I'm worried that you're not here, but that's stupid because these films are supposed to be the lives of everyone in the cinema. So I start exploring round the auditorium looking for you . . . this is the place.'

'What?'

'This is where we're going. You have to go up on that escalator.'

'Here? What is this, a cinema?'

'No, it's not a cinema. Stop guessing, you'll understand in a minute. Go on, go up.'

She shoved him up the steps. He leaned back onto her hands, letting her push.

'Tell me the end of your dream.'

'OK, well, usually the dream ends with me trying to escape from the cinema. I run across to one of the fire exits, but no matter how hard I try to stay asleep, I always wake up before I can open the door. But last night, I found you in the audience . . . that was the best bit of the dream, I always like walking around in cinemas when the audience are engrossed . . . and managed to enlist you in my quest, and we got to the door and opened it and . . .'

'What?'

'I don't know, I woke up.'

Chris sighed.

'But at least I managed to open the door. Don't you see . . . that's really important.'

He ignored her. 'What is this place? An ice-rink?'

'Yeah.'

'But it's closed.'

'That doesn't matter, go up to the doors.'

'Why?'

'Look, you'll just have to trust me. Besides, you said you wanted to go ice-skating.'

'When?'

'Last time we went out.'

'I don't remember.'

'It doesn't matter. But you can skate, can't you?'

'Of course I can. I have certificates.'

'Certificates? For ice-skating?'

'Yeah, you know, there's one for skating backwards, another for jumping over a chair.'

'Well, you won't be doing any chair-jumping today. Now, go and ring the bell.'

Chris did as she instructed. A pale-faced girl with a row of pimples along her upper lip unlocked the door.

'Yes?' she asked.

Chris pointed at Becca. 'She sent me.'

The girl looked over, nodded, and then stepped back. Becca gestured for Chris to go inside. He did, and the girl asked him,

'What size?'

'Nines,' he said, walking over to a seating area and taking off his shoes.

The girl looked at Becca.

'Six,' she said, coming over and sitting alongside Chris.

The girl walked across to a locked area, which she opened with a key and then went inside, walking back across with two pairs of skates. They handed across their shoes, and Becca looked out to the ice.

'Is this nice?' she asked.

'It's fantastic, thanks.'

They stood up together and hobbled towards the rink. It had been ages since Becca last skated, but it soon came back to her. Chris was smoother and faster, and looked more natural on the ice. Becca'd never quite been able to get rid of the habit of trying to walk instead of skating, and although she'd adapted that into her style, it still looked a little strange.

They stayed on the ice for almost an hour, both enjoying the luxury of having the whole rink to themselves. At the end of their time, the girl came to the edge of the rink and gestured at them to come off. Chris swooped straight down the centre of the ice, leaping onto the wet plastic mat at the edge of the rink. Becca returned in a much more gentle way, going round one more time and then slowly skating in towards the side, stepping up onto the mat when she reached a gap in the wall that surrounded the ice.

'Well,' she said, catching her breath, 'that was fun, wasn't it?'

Chris nodded. 'And a complete surprise. Thank you.'

'Do you want to know what the other options were?' she asked, taking the paper diamond from her pocket.

'No,' he said. 'I'm sure they can't have been as great as this has been.'

'Well,' she conceded, 'this was probably the most extravagant.'

'How am I going to top this next time we go out?'

'Oh, come on, Chris, this isn't about oneupmanship. It's about fun.'

'I know,' he said. 'I was only joking.'

They changed back into their shoes and left the rink. Becca went to the toilet and when she came back the girl was waiting, eager to lock up behind them. Her legs felt wobbly and Chris looked at the damp patches at the bottom of his trousers.

'I suppose you have to get back now?'

She nodded. 'I'm sorry.'

'Should I even try to persuade you to come back to my place?'

She put her fingers over his lips. 'Don't. Don't spoil it.'

'OK,' he shrugged, 'but thanks for today anyway.'

She smiled. 'I don't understand why you keep getting so sad. You'll see me again soon. Don't you like this?'

'Of course I like this. I'd just like something more permanent.'

'Well,' she said, 'you'll just have to wait and see. Who knows what might happen.'

He looked at her again, saying in a churlish voice, 'You're mean to me.'

'I set up a surprise afternoon and take you ice-skating and you think that's mean? I should have taken you to Burger King.'

'You know what I mean.'

She walked across and took his arm, using a finger to press his lips into a smile. Becca smiled at him and he held her gaze for a moment. Turning his head away, Chris said,

'Do you remember where the bus stop was?'

She laughed. 'Of course. Don't you?'
He shook his head. 'Lead the way.'

'So what do you think?'

Chris looked down at the neat pile of pages stacked in front of him. He'd been unable to persuade Andy's brother to leave his flat while he read his screenplay, and he'd spent the last two hours waiting for Chris to get to the end.

'What exactly do you want from me?' Chris asked.

'Your opinion. Do you think it's funny? You didn't laugh once.'

Chris turned round from the desk. 'No, it is funny. But like I said, I don't know that much about selling screenplays so it's hard to know how to advise you. If you need help finding an agent I can probably do that, but I think you need to work on it a bit more first. For a start, your layout is very unconventional.'

'You mean how the plot develops?'

'No, I mean how it looks on the page. I think you should probably buy a book on how to format a screenplay. Or get that *First Draft* software.'

Andy's brother seemed insulted by this advice. 'But what did you think of the story?'

'Um . . . it's certainly a very interesting concept. And the set-up is very well done. I like pretty much all of it until the baby gets to Vietnam.'

'That's only the first ten pages.'

Chris looked through. 'True, but I don't hate the rest. I just found it a little disturbing . . . the mixture of the violence and the adult humour and the baby . . . I mean, I could see how it could work, if you had the right director, but . . .'

'It's going to be an animatronic baby.'

'Pardon?'

'I don't think they should use a real baby. If they have an animatronic one they can do better special effects.'

'Yes, I suppose they could. Actually, knowing that makes me feel a little differently about the whole thing.'

'Do you want to read it again?'

'What?'

'Do you want to read it again? Now you know it's going to be a puppet baby. Like Chucky. I can hang around for a bit.'

'No,' said Chris, 'I will read it again, but not right now. If you leave it here, I can look it over tonight and get back to you tomorrow.'

'I'm afraid I can't do that.'

'What?'

'Leave the script. It's not that I don't trust you. And I know that you and my brother go way back. But . . . I just can't do it.'

Chris sighed, still unsure how he'd got mixed up in this madness.

'OK,' he said, 'take it. I'm sorry I wasn't more help.'

'No, no,' replied Andy's brother, shaking his head. 'It's been good just getting you to read it. It's such a relief, you know, just to get these ideas out of my head.'

'I understand. I feel like that with my articles sometimes.'

'But not a word to my brother, OK?' he said, standing up. 'Promise?'

'Of course,' said Chris, handing him back the manuscript. 'Good luck.'

You always have to tell one person.

You always have to tell one person, and that's almost always a mistake. But that was the rule, and there was no point her trying to pretend that wasn't the case. You always have to tell one person, and if you don't choose who to tell, then the secret will just come out anyway, and usually at the most inappropriate moment.

The obvious person was Scarlett. Everyone told their secrets to Scarlett, and even though she had the reputation of being notoriously indiscreet, this usually proved not to be the case, mainly because Scarlett had her own reasons for wanting to keep everybody together. But Scarlett didn't seem right for this secret, and Becca had never been able to completely shake the notion that she harboured fond feelings for James, and didn't want to give her this ammunition.

But if she ruled out Scarlett, who did that leave? Becca didn't have that many close friends, and the few that she did have were friends with James as well. No, she needed someone who'd have no feelings of divided loyalty. She wanted someone who was completely on her side. Or, better still, someone who'd never met James at all.

Once she'd reached that conclusion, her choice of confidante was obvious.

'So what's up?' Jessica asked as she slid into the empty chair.

'Nothing serious,' said Becca. 'I just had something I wanted to talk to you about. It's to do with the flat.'

'OK.'

'Or rather, it's do with my tenant.'

'Chris.'

'Yeah.' Just hearing his name made her blush. 'Well . . .'

Jessica laughed, shocked. 'Oh my God, Becca, where did you meet him?'

'Shall we order first?'

Their usual waiter was hovering by the table. They ordered their food and he asked if they wanted anything to drink.

'What d'you reckon?' she asked Jessica. 'Are you up to sharing a bottle? This really is a sharing-a-bottle story.'

'Hang on,' said Jessica, taking her diary from her bag and placing it on the table, 'I just want to check who I've got coming in this afternoon.'

Becca looked away as she flipped through a few pages.

'Duncan, he'll be OK. And . . . yeah, go on then, I'll join you.'

The waiter nodded, and walked away.

'Who's Duncan?'

'This guy from Scotland with an incredibly large head. He's very charming, and quite camp, but it's hard not to stare at him.'

'Because of his head?'

She nodded. 'It's terrible.'

'And will he mind you being a bit giggly?'

'I shouldn't think so. And anyway, I got drunk with him once before so he shouldn't be too worried.'

'Is that standard estate agent practice?'

'You don't want to know about standard estate agent practice. Let's just say, you remember what your last estate agent did?'

'The pig?'

'Yeah. Well, that's standard estate agent practice.'

*

Their wine arrived. Becca told Jessica everything. Total disclosure, that was the only way to do it. That meant that there was nothing left to sneak out later; no detail that might force its own audience. By the time she'd reached the end of her story, they'd finished the food, and the wine, and were left contemplating dessert, coffee, or another bottle.

'What d'you reckon? Another bottle?'

'Um . . .' Jessica took her mobile from her bag. 'Maybe. Just let me make a couple of calls.'

Becca nodded, listened to her rearrange her appointment with Duncan, and then went to the toilet as Jessica called someone else. When she came back, there was a fresh bottle on the table.

'So what happens next?' Jessica asked.

'Now, you mean?'

'No, with Chris.'

'I'm stopping.'

'What?'

'I've decided I can't see him any more.'

'But why? You've just spent two hours telling me how wonderful he is.'

'Exactly.'

'I don't understand.'

'If I carry on seeing Chris, I'm never going to be happy with James again.'

'Then leave James.'

'I can't.'

'Why not?'

She started crying, quiet tears with no accompanying sobs. 'Because I love him.'

'Do you?'

'Yes,' she said, 'and besides, even if I did leave James, how could I explain to Chris that I've spent all this time spying on him.'

'I'm sure he'd understand.'

'You don't know that. Imagine for a minute if it was the other way round. Suppose you started going out with a guy, and then discovered that before you'd started going out together, he'd been stalking you.'

'Well, you're right, that does sound a little creepy. But you've hardly been stalking this guy.'

'What else would you call it?'

'I don't know. But you shouldn't let that stop you. And so what if he freaks out? He'll calm down eventually.'

Jessica pushed her hair out of her eyes and looked directly at Becca.

'Becca,' she said.

'Yes?'

'Have you done this before?'

Becca looked at Jessica. She couldn't work out why she'd always thought of her estate agent as a weak woman. Some of her superiority came from the fact that Jessica was working for her, but she'd also made other assumptions based on the way she dressed and talked. Now she regretted not properly befriending her, and realised it'd been arrogance that'd made her believe that Jessica found her company stressful.

'No, of course not.'

'Well then, what are you worried about? Everyone does this sort of thing. Look, I get those same sorts of urges sometimes.'

'But you don't sneak into people's houses.'

'No, that's true. They normally give me the keys in advance. But, look, you're not interested in justifying this to everyone. You're interested in justifying this to Chris. And I know I don't know him as well as you do, but my impression of him is that he's not the kind of guy who's going to be freaked out by this.'

'And if he is?'

'Well, then you've still got James. I realise that's a pretty callous way of looking at it, but it makes more sense than not even giving him a chance to see if he understands.'

Becca nodded. 'You're right.'

'I know. And you wait and see. Everything will turn out exactly the way you want it to.'

It'd been Scarlett's idea to follow James.

She'd been extremely sympathetic when Chris had called her, calming him down after he'd angrily blurted out that he and Becca would no longer be seeing each other. She'd even managed to persuade him not to go storming round to Becca's house, making him understand that it made more sense to find out what he was up against. And it was only after she'd put the phone down that she gave a second thought to the wisdom of giving Chris the address of James' workplace.

Chris only had to wait half an hour or so before James left his agency for lunch. From the little Becca had said Chris had formed the impression that he should be on the lookout for a conservative guy in a smart suit. So he almost missed James when he came out of the office wearing a light blue jacket and a grey T-shirt. In fact, he wouldn't have realised at all had not a ginger-haired girl in an ugly green fleece followed James outside and called after him.

James turned and smiled at the girl. They talked for a while, but not in a manner that suggested anything illicit was going on between them. Then the girl went back into the office and James turned away and started walking in the opposite direction. Chris followed him for a while, staying on the other side of the road. He let James draw ahead and then crossed so he was walking behind him.

He followed James onto Lexington Street. James stopped outside The Lexington restaurant, and then pushed open the door and walked inside. Chris hesitated, nervous about following him. He kept thinking that James would somehow recognise him, even though they'd never met before.

He let a few minutes pass, then entered the restaurant himself. James was sitting at a table near the toilets, alone. Chris let the waitress guide him to the table opposite him. She asked him if he'd like a drink and he ordered a bottle of mineral water and a beer.

He looked at the menu, then went back to watching James. He could tell he was waiting for someone from the way he kept looking at his watch.

The waitress returned with Chris's beer. He filled the glass with water and drank a first swallow of beer.

'Are you ready to order?' the woman asked.

Chris nodded. 'I'll have the mussels and the steak.'

'Sure.'

She walked away. Chris watched James stand up, although he couldn't see who'd entered until she'd walked right over to the opposite table. Then he recognised her immediately, even though she had her back to him.

It was Diana.

Chris now felt extremely awkward. He'd known all along that this was a stupid idea. Although Scarlett had insisted this definitely didn't count as stalking, it was hard to know how else to describe what he was doing. And while it didn't matter when he was only tailing someone he'd never met, now that Diana was here she was bound to think he was following her. It would be different if he was meeting someone, but as he was dining alone, Diana was bound to find it creepy.

Unless . . .

While Diana still had her back to him, he sneaked out from his seat and went down to the telephone.

'Scarlett?' he said.

'Yes?' she answered.

'You anywhere near Soho?'

She laughed. 'How d'you guess? Soho House, as a matter of fact. Why?'

'I need you to come to the Lexington immediately.'

'The restaurant?'

'Yes.'

'Why?'

'I'll explain when you arrive. But you have to come this minute.'

He heard her say something to the people she was with, and then she said,

'How long will I be?'

'About an hour. But, listen, I'm going to buy you lunch.'

'Sounds fair. OK, see you in a few minutes.'

He hung up and went back to his table. Diana had now sat down, still with her back towards him, and she still hadn't noticed him. Chris sat down at his table and beckoned the waitress. She came across.

'I'm sorry to cause trouble, but could you hold back my food?' he told her. 'I want to keep the same order, but I've just spoken with a friend who'll be joining me shortly.'

'That's fine, sir.'

She walked away. Chris poured himself another glass of water.

James was the first to notice Scarlett. It was hard to know how well he knew her from his reaction, but once he'd pointed her out to Diana, she stood up, turned around, embraced her and kissed her on both cheeks.

'Who are you with?' he heard Diana ask Scarlett.

Scarlett pointed at Chris. Chris smiled at Diana, anxious about how she might react. He couldn't believe they'd run into each other so soon after their split. He'd assumed the next time he'd see her would be on TV, not at a restaurant with the boyfriend of a woman with whom he was having a secret affair.

'Chris,' said Diana, her tone neutral. She held his gaze for a moment, before a slight smile formed on her lips. 'Small world.'

Chris checked out the two women looking at him. Usually he couldn't help feeling awkward in these situations, and was the kind of person who always seemed to be placed slightly off-centre in all the serious scenes. And that was how he would have felt now if he hadn't persuaded Scarlett across Soho to join him. But with her here, the scene seemed perfect.

Diana was wearing a light cream cardigan over a grey top and a short, checked skirt. They were clothes he remembered from her wardrobe, but they were also items with no particular associations, which made him feel relieved. They also didn't seem especially obvious date clothes, and this also pleased Chris, at least until he remembered that the first time they went out together she'd shown up in jeans and a T-shirt.

'Would you like to join us?' Diana asked Scarlett.

She looked at Chris. 'No, that's OK. I always feel a bit cramped when there's more than two people around a table.'

Diana nodded. 'I know what you mean. But, look, Scarlett, call me, OK?'

'Of course.'

They separated, and Scarlett came across to join Chris. She raised her eyebrows and smiled at him. Then she pulled out her chair and sat down.

'OK, Chris, what's going on?'

'Stalking James.'

'Oh right,' she said, 'I see. So you didn't realise Diana would be here?'

'No, of course not. Do you think I want to sit here and watch my ex-girlfriend while she's out on a date?'

'I don't know. Some men go for that sort of thing.'

He glared at her.

'OK,' she said, 'I'm sorry. Don't get all grumpy. What's your next move?'

'What d'you mean?'

'Surely you haven't given up. This is exactly what you need.'

'You think I should tell Becca that her boyfriend is having an affair?'

'I didn't say that.'

'Look, I don't know if this is anything. And, besides, she's hardly going to appreciate me telling her, is she?'

'You don't have to tell her. And, anyway, it doesn't matter whether this is an affair or not. All that's important is that you know he's as dissatisfied with their relationship as she is. Now you don't have to feel guilty about putting the pressure on.'

'So you're saying I should find Becca?'

'Maybe. Or maybe you should find out how she's feeling first. It's all about picking your moment.'

Chris nodded. 'Thanks, Scarlett, that's good advice.'

'Oh, come on, Chris, please cheer up. I promise you, I have good feelings about this. You two were made for each other.'

She smiled, and Chris took her hands across the table, pleased to have called upon the right friend this time round.

Chris's Favourite Films #2

After Hours

Andy and Chris often talked about whether it was a good thing that Scorsese had directed *After Hours*. It seemed good because as usual he did such a fantastic job, giving Minion's script the perfect execution. Without Scorsese's direction, the film could've lapsed into the simply weird, like the truly bonkers Minion movie *Motorama*, or the *After Hours* cast reunion project, *Search and Destroy*. But, on the other hand, the fact that it was a Scorsese movie somehow made it uncool. Not that Scorsese was uncool . . . he was very cool. But somehow liking his movies wasn't.

The other problem with it being a Scorsese movie was that because he was so many people's favourite director, there was already an established set of rules about which of his films were good and which were crap. Unless you were prepared to risk ridicule, the accepted orthodoxy about Scorsese was that his best films had De Niro in them. *Raging Bull* or *Taxi Driver* was the best, then *Goodfellas* and *Mean Streets*, with *Casino* and *Cape Fear* a little way behind. Then there were the De Niro films that supposedly didn't work, like *New York, New York* and *The King of Comedy* (and here again Chris didn't fall into step as the latter was his second favourite Scorsese film). Then came his less personal projects, like *The Colour of Money, After Hours* and his segment of *New York Stories*. Followed by the religious films (*Kundun, The Last Temptation of Christ*), the disappointments (*Bringing Out the Dead, The Age of Innocence*) and the curios (*The Last Waltz, Boxcar Bertha, Alice Doesn't Live Here Anymore*). And, much as he loved *After Hours*, Chris couldn't be bothered to argue why a small, quiet comedy was better than the accepted classics.

This didn't stop him thinking about scenes from the film almost every day. *After Hours* was the only film he'd seen that seemed utterly realistic, every scene something Chris had already experienced. The bit in the bar, where John Heard can't open the till to lend Griffin Dunne change and Dunne says it's OK and Heard asks what he's supposed to do when the other customers come in. Or the opening scene, where Dunne is so bored by his co-worker's plans to start a literary magazine that he can't even look at him. These moments seemed like memories from his own life, which seemed the highest compliment you could pay a film.

One of the only things Chris had over Andy was that he had introduced him to *After Hours*. Chris was fairly sure it was Andy's number one movie, and whenever they talked about favourite films, he got a sadistic pleasure out of keeping it at number two.

They'd agreed to meet at Tower Records in Piccadilly Circus. Becca found Scarlett by the magazine rack, flipping through a copy of *Dazed and Confused*.

'Look,' said Scarlett, showing her the magazine, 'there's a piece on Stephen.'

Becca leaned over and looked at the piece Scarlett was pointing to. 'Is he in your film too?'

'No. I don't think they offered it to him. Fuck knows why, he would've been perfect for it. And he's still too much of a newcomer to turn stuff down.'

'What stage is the film at?'

'Oh, it's all done now. The shooting, I mean. They're about to start editing.'

'Cool. Have you decided where you want to go?'

'I don't have long, I'm afraid. Shall we just go for a quick coffee at the Trocadero?'

'OK.'

Becca waited while Scarlett went up to the till to pay for her magazine. She felt less nervous than she had done before she'd come out, but was still curious about what Scarlett wanted from her. At first she'd assumed that she was going to offer her a job, but if the film was wrapped that probably wasn't going to happen. Unless she was about to get involved with a new project.

She watched Scarlett walk back towards her. She'd known lots of women like Scarlett in her life. Extremely confident, fun, exciting women who didn't seem tethered to the world in the same way she was, managing to make light of the problems that she would brood about for days. Scarlett looked especially attractive today, wearing a flattering white top and a long skirt.

They went through the exit that took them into Piccadilly Station and then back up the steps and past HMV. They took the escalator to the first floor of the Trocadero and went into the café there. Becca waited by the counter while Scarlett got them two coffees and carried them across to a metal table where they sat down together.

'So what did you want to talk to me about?'

'A few things. Nothing serious. How are things between you and Chris?'

Becca sipped her coffee and looked at Scarlett, wondering how to answer her question. Now she understood why she was here: Chris had clearly asked Scarlett to persuade her not to break things off with him. Touched, she decided to be more open with Scarlett than she was usually. No doubt it would all get back to Chris, but maybe this was the best way to explain herself. Much less messy than taking care of things face to face.

'They're over. We had a couple of nice dates . . . the first one was wonderful, the second one was a bit weird, but that was more my fault than his . . .'

'How come?'

'It's really stupid. I'm embarrassed to tell you.'

Her smile widened. 'Go on.'

'You know those paper things kids make in school? Those pick a colour, pick a number things?'

Scarlett nodded.

'Well, I made one of those and on the inside flaps I wrote all my favourite romantic scenes from the movies. You know, *Officer and a Gentleman*, *One Fine Day*, things like that. It would've been fine, but he picked the weirdest one.'

'Which was?'

'*Rocky*.'

'What?'

Becca laughed. 'I know, I know, but it was all because of that weirdo at your party.'

'What weirdo?'

'The screenwriter. Joel. You remember when we came up to you and asked if you had a film guide?'

'Yeah.'

'Well, the reason we wanted one was because we were playing this stupid game when you had to guess what year certain films came out. And he asked me to do all the Rocky movies.'

'I don't even remember there being a romantic scene in *Rocky*. Did Chris have to pretend to be a boxer while you begged him not to fight?'

'No, you do remember, it's the bit where Rocky asks Adrienne what she likes to do and she says she likes ice-skating so he takes her, but when he gets there the rink is shut, so he has to slip the owner some money to let them out onto the ice.'

'So you took Chris ice-skating?'

'Yeah.'

'That's nice.' Scarlett reached down into her bag and took out a small rectangular box wrapped in pink paper. 'Look, Becca, I don't even know if I'm doing the right thing, but I want to tell you that the only reason I'm doing this is that I've been in this situation so many times before, and no one's ever told me what's going on, even my best friends.'

'Slow down,' said Becca, struggling to process Scarlett's words. 'Is this about me and Chris?'

'In a way, yes. But I need to start off with a couple of confessions.'

Becca sat back. 'OK.'

'That night at the Prince Charles was completely set up. I got you to come as Molly Ringwald and told Chris to dress up as Judd Nelson.'

Becca tried not to laugh at her serious expression. 'That's not that much of a surprise, Scarlett.'

'OK. When you told Chris you weren't going to see him any more, he phoned me up.'

'I thought that might've happened. Is that what this is about?'

'In a way. Before I tell you the next bit, let me give you this.' She handed across the box.

'What is it?'

'Every girl's best friend.'

'Not a . . .'

'No,' said Scarlett quickly, 'I'm not that crass. Anyway, when Chris called me I gave him some advice that's actually turned out to be pretty stupid.'

'What?'

'I told him to follow James.' Her voice dropped into quiet sincerity. 'I don't really know why. I guess it was probably because he was really vulnerable, and having that connection with you, even though it was unlikely to lead to anything, was helping him get over Diana.'

'I met her.'

'Diana?'

'Yeah.'

'At my party, you mean?'

'No, after that. I went for a drink with her.'

'How come?'

'James persuaded her to put me forward for a job on her TV show.'

'Did you get the job?'

'Yeah. I mean, they offered it to me, but I turned it down.'

Scarlett nodded. 'Well, that's sort of what this is about. The other day Chris was following James, and he saw him in a restaurant with Diana. I know it's true, I saw him too, he spoke to me. Maybe he mentioned it.'

Becca shook her head.

'I'm sure it's nothing, and I'm not trying to shit-stir, really I'm not, but I just thought, seeing as you're giving up Chris, you deserve to know about it. If you want you could just ask him. Say you spoke to me and I told you.'

'OK, I'll do that.' She picked up the box. 'But tell me what's in here.'

'Something to guide you. And, remember, Melanie's never anybody's girl.'

Scarlett's cryptic comment at least started to make sense when Becca got home and discovered her friend had given her a copy of *Working Girl*. She assumed it wasn't a reference to the title, and was a comment instead on how Melanie rarely played second fiddle in her films, always assuming the lead role. She also wondered about Scarlett's remark that this was 'every girl's best friend' and wondered whether she was trying to give her a message through the film. Although she'd watched it a couple of times when it'd first come out, the movie wasn't really one of her favourites and she decided she needed to watch it again to understand why Scarlett had wanted her to have this video.

She checked the clock, wanting to make sure she had time to watch the film before James came home. Satisfied she had long enough, she slid the tape into her video and pressed play. She'd forgotten Kevin Spacey was in the film, and remembering that he was one of Scarlett's favourite actors, she wondered if she'd wanted her to take note of the scene he was in. But neither Chris nor James was particularly slimy, and even if James had been unfaithful, she could think of much more sophisticated plans for revenge than tipping champagne into his lap.

And neither had Chris been unfaithful, like Alec Baldwin. So maybe it was Harrison Ford she was supposed to be focusing on. She'd never been a big fan of the actor, having found him bland from *American Graffiti* onwards. But she had to admit the scene where he first ran into Melanie was fun, and as she proceeded to get so drunk that he had to carry her home over his shoulder, a connection clicked.

She found the phone and called Scarlett.

'I get it.'

'How's my favourite love-sick teenager?'

'OK,' said Chris, remembering how helpful Scarlett had been in the Lexington and trying not to get annoyed. Most of the time he was grateful that Scarlett had taken a special interest in him, but there were times, like today, when he couldn't help thinking that she was enjoying his emotional turmoil. 'I hope you're calling with good news.'

'Then you're going to be very pleased. Do you have a pen?'

'Hang on . . . yeah.'

'Right, now the place is called the Piano Bar and it's in Yarmouth Place behind the Japanese Embassy. The nearest tube, I think, is Hyde Park Corner, and you have to get there for ten o'clock.'

He was about to ask why when he realised she'd hung up.

Becca checked herself in the mirror. She had to admit Scarlett was good at this. And since her film had finished shooting, all of her attention seemed to have gone into stage-managing the developments between her and Chris.

'Scarlett,' she said as she raised a large pair of earrings to her ear, 'are you seeing anyone at the moment?'

She shook her head. 'No. There was someone on the film who was interested in me, but I kind of screwed it up.'

Becca looked at Scarlett. 'That doesn't fill me with confidence.'

Scarlett took a lipstick from the dressing-table. 'Relax, it's only my own relationships I can't sort out. Open your lips.'

Becca reached for Scarlett's hand. 'I'm already wearing lipstick.'

'Are you? Well, it's far too subtle.' She handed her a tissue. 'And, besides, who else is going to help you? I like you, I like Chris, I just want to see you work things out.'

'And you're sure you saw James with Diana?'

'I told you, I spoke to them.'

'I know, but I've been thinking about this. Maybe he was just taking Diana to lunch to thank her for fixing me up with an interview at ColourMePink.'

'Maybe, but that doesn't change any of this. The whole point of this evening is to test both men. Then you can see who comes out of this best. Besides, if his lunch with Diana was entirely innocent, don't you think he would've told you about it by now?'

'What time did you tell Chris to come?' Becca asked Scarlett as they settled themselves in the Piano Bar.

'Ten. So you've got two and a half hours to get yourself plastered. Which should be easy. Melanie Griffiths manages it in about three minutes.'

'Yeah, I thought that was weird. Why is it that drink and drugs scenes in films are always so unrealistic? I mean, it's not exactly a subject celebrities don't know about.'

'Maybe that's the point. They want us to think they can only *act* being drunk. Now, come on, you won't get pissed by spending all night talking. What do you want to start with?'

'I don't know, something naughty. Something I used to drink when I was a kid. How about a rum and Coke?'

'OK.' She walked to the bar. Becca watched Scarlett order the drinks, amazed at herself for still going along with such a stupid idea. It was raining outside, and Becca began to wonder if this was the most sensible place to get drunk. She didn't understand why Becca had chosen somewhere in Mayfair, apart from the fact that if she got hassle it would probably come from men in suits.

Scarlett sat back down and gave Becca her drink.

'OK, girl, down in one.'

Chris took out his *A–Z*. He'd hoped he wouldn't need it, but he was sure he should've reached the Japanese Embassy by this point, and decided to stop and check before he walked too far in the wrong direction. He had to admit that he was quite enjoying his latest adventure, and his only regret was that it wasn't more elaborate, a mystery involving cloaks, a Beethoven opera and seventies-style prostitutes. Even having to walk in the rain didn't particularly bother him, and for the early part of his journey, he'd enjoyed pretending he was being followed and that he was attempting to shake off an imaginary pursuer.

Looking at the map, he realised his mistake and headed back down the road he was on. After that, it was only one street to the Piano Bar. Seeing Becca through the window increased his excitement, and he rushed inside. She didn't notice him until he was right next to her, putting his wet hand on her back.

'Becca . . .'

She turned round, smiling warmly at him. He could tell something was wrong, but didn't yet know what. She seemed happy in a miserable way, and he wondered whether this was because she'd left James.

'Chris,' she said, 'thanks for coming.'

'Scarlett didn't tell me you'd be here. I didn't know what to expect.' He looked down at her empty glass. 'Can I get you something to drink?'

'God, no . . . can you just wait here a moment?'

'Of course.'

She stood up. She was dressed in a much more extravagant

fashion than she'd been on any of their previous dates. He remembered Twelve Hour Teens and wondered whether Scarlett had persuaded her to dress up again. Then he noticed that she was extremely unsteady and realised she was drunk. He immediately felt anxious, aware of how bad he was at handling situations like this. Part of him wondered whether it would be best to just leave. But he felt a moral responsibility to make sure she was OK.

He walked to the bar and ordered himself a beer. The bartender smiled at him. After a while, Chris turned to where Becca had been sitting and said,

'That woman I'm with. Has she been here long?'

The waiter looked at his watch. 'Most of the evening.'

'Alone?'

'No, she was with another girl for most of the night. She left about fifteen minutes ago.'

Scarlett. Well, she must've had a reason for filling Becca with booze. Feeling mystified, he went back to his seat. Ten minutes passed. He began to get worried, wondering if Becca had found some way of slipping out the back. The bartender looked at him at the same moment, and came out to join him. Without exchanging a word, the two of them went into the ladies' toilet.

They found Becca slumped in the second cubicle. She didn't seem to have been that extravagantly sick, but at some point had tried to crawl into the small space between the wall and the pedestal.

'Can you get her home?' the bartender asked.

'I think so.'

The bartender leaned down and helped Becca up to her feet. Chris tried to look sturdy as the bartender hooked Becca round his neck. He gripped her waist and walked her out of the cubicle. The bartender leaned back against the wall. Chris stopped to hand him a ten-pound note.

The bartender smiled. 'Thank you, sir.'

As soon as he got her outside, Chris realised there was no way he could get her home on the tube. No regular cabdriver would take a passenger in her state, so . . . it was time to call Andy's brother.

Surprised to find an occasion when he was grateful for this connection, Chris helped Becca into a telephone box and dialled the memorised number. Andy's brother told Chris he could get to Mayfair in fifteen minutes.

'Great,' said Chris after hearing this good news. 'There is one slight problem.'

'Yeah?'

'I have Becca with me. She's a bit the worse for wear.'

'Don't worry,' he replied, 'I'll bring a bucket.'

After a few minutes waiting in the rain, Becca began to wake up. Chris could tell she was horrified.

'Is my dress OK?' she asked.

'You weren't sick on it if that's what you mean. Although you were on the toilet floor for a while.'

'Oh God,' she groaned, 'I knew this was a bad idea.'

'One of Scarlett's?'

'How d'you guess?'

'The bartender said you'd come with a friend.'

'I'm sorry, Chris, I know you hate drunk women.'

'What?' he asked, shocked. 'Did Scarlett say that?'

She shook her head. 'Diana.'

'My Diana?'

Becca closed her eyes. 'This is all too complicated to explain now. Can you just help me get home?'

'Of course. The taxi's on its way. But I thought you might like to come home with me.'

'I don't think that's a good idea.'

'Not to do anything. Just to sober up. Or if you want to stay, that's fine too. You can call your boyfriend and say you're staying with Scarlett.'

'That's really kind of you ... but I want to be in my bed. Hangovers are always easier if you're in your own home.'

He nodded. 'I understand.'

They waited in silence until Andy's brother arrived. He was in an exuberant mood, getting out of his taxi and coming over to help Becca into the back. She clutched at his dirty cream jacket as he lowered her onto the seat.

'Hectic night?' he asked.

'Yeah,' Chris replied, not feeling up to a conversation.

'So where are we going?'

Becca gave him her address.

'OK. Anyone mind if I put the radio on?'

Chris didn't say anything to Becca until they'd reached her house, and Andy's brother had got out of the cab to go round and open her door.

'Look, Becca, we can't leave things like this. I have to see you again.'

She shook her head. 'It's too depressing. And embarrassing. I know the next time we meet we're going to have to rehash all this.'

'No, it's fine, we don't have to talk about it. Meet me at Bar Italia, OK? Monday, three o'clock.'

'I'm not sure.'

'Please.'

Andy's brother opened the taxi door. Becca kissed Chris and got out.

James was sitting in the lounge, watching television. Becca had asked Chris not to come with her to the door, and she'd had some trouble with her key. Stopping to take her shoes off, she walked over behind James.

'How was Scarlett?' he asked.

'OK.' She crossed to the kitchen. 'You didn't tell me you ran into her.'

'When?'

Becca went into the kitchen, immediately striding to the sink and pouring herself a large glass of water. She looked through the cupboard, knowing she should eat something and wondering what'd be the best thing to stave off a hangover.

'She said she saw you in a restaurant. With that girl from the party.'

He didn't say anything. She found a piece of bread and returned to the lounge. Becca knew it was dangerous to approach a confrontation in this state, but still felt angry about mucking things up with Chris, and was determined to reach some sort of resolution.

'Right, yeah, I had lunch with Diana.'

'And how come you didn't say anything?'

'It didn't really occur to me. We didn't really say much to each other.'

'Have you seen Diana since then?'

'Why would I see her?'

'I don't know. Why did you see her the first time?'

'No real reason. I just got on with her at the party and thought I'd like her as a friend. Is that not OK with you?'

Becca suddenly felt tired and sat down too quickly. James got up and peered at her.

'Are you OK?'

'I'm fine.' She sipped from her glass of water, aware this was a giveaway and deciding to turn herself in. 'Just a bit pissed.'

James got up and came over next to her. 'Is this because of Diana?'

'Is what because of Diana?'

'That you're drunk.'

'No, I just couldn't keep up with Scarlett.'

He nodded. 'OK, well, let me help you upstairs.' He lifted her up. 'Bring your bread and water.'

And although she wanted to struggle, Becca found it too comforting to be held, falling asleep the moment James dropped her onto the bed.

Becca's Dodgy Boyfriends #5
Craig

Between Jason and James, Becca had a brief fling with a guy who was five years younger than her. He claimed to be a DJ, but in the whole time she went out with him she never saw him buy a single record and they only went clubbing three times, going to a tiny venue in south London that looked less like a club than someone's living room.

The relationship ended after an argument where she asked him why he didn't have a proper DJ name, like 3D or Squarepusher or Fatboy Slim. He said he wasn't that sort of DJ, so she asked him if he was a DJ like the blokes from the Chemical Brothers, and he told her that was like comparing him to Cliff Richard and stormed out of her flat. She wasn't sad to see him go, and didn't make any effort to get him back.

Chris sat nursing a coffee outside Bar Italia, waiting for Becca to show up. She was already almost an hour late, and although he was below one of the large outdoor heaters he was nevertheless beginning to feel the cold. Usually he quite liked being here, finding it romantic. But even before he had stepped out of his house today he'd had the feeling that Becca might not show, and was now worried his premonition was about to come true. He finished the last of his coffee, and wondered whether it was worth going inside for another.

He decided against it, taking his coat from the back of his chair and crossing the road. Feeling disappointed and upset, he caught the tube home and wondered what had gone wrong.

When he got back to his flat, he checked his ansaphone, still prepared to forgive her if she'd left an explanation. But there was nothing there, not even a message from someone else. These sort of clandestine relationships never worked if they got turned into power-struggles, and although so far they'd managed to avoid that, he couldn't help worrying that this was the beginning of the end.

She called at ten-thirty. Chris didn't feel like talking to her, but after letting the machine answer the first time, he picked up the phone when she called again five minutes later.

'I knew you were there,' she said, breathing into the mouthpiece.

'So what happened?'

'I'm sorry, Chris, don't be cross.'

'Why didn't you show up?'

'I couldn't. It's complicated. It really couldn't be helped.'

'Fine.'

He waited for her to continue. He could tell she was getting irritated and upset, but didn't feel like being lenient, and was still cross and embarrassed about spending an hour alone in Bar Italia.

'Please don't be angry. Look, I called because something's changed.'

'You've left your boyfriend?'

'No. But I think I'm ready to come to your house.'

'Why?'

'Huh?'

'What's made you ready?'

'You.'

'I don't understand. Has this got something to do with today?'

'Maybe it's a bad idea.'

'Oh God, that's so unfair. I am allowed to be upset, you know. It was cruel of you to stand me up.'

'I know, I'm sorry.'

'It's OK. And I'd love for you to come to my house.'

'Great. Is tomorrow afternoon OK?'

'That would be perfect.'

'Three o'clock?'

'Fine.'

She didn't say goodbye, but he could tell from the noise at the other end of the line that she'd hung up. Confused, Chris walked back into his study and sat at his desk, wondering what Becca had meant when she'd said something had changed, and realising that he'd have to spend at least the next few hours tidying up.

Becca was determined to be on time. In fact, she'd decided to be a few minutes early, to make up for yesterday's waiting. She arrived at Chris's place at two forty-five, and then, worried he might be watching from his window, nipped into the pub at the end of the street and downed a quick vodka tonic. Ten minutes later, she was at his front door.

Instead of buzzing her in, he came down to the front door. She found this sweet, and kissed him on both cheeks.

The place was much tidier than the two times she'd sneaked in here alone. Even if he was only doing it to please her, Becca felt relieved. He asked for her coat and she handed it to him.

'I like your shoes,' he said.

She looked at him, surprised. It seemed an odd thing for him to compliment. She liked her shoes too, although they weren't expensive or particularly stylish. Blue sandals with a closed toe and raised heel, they weren't really appropriate for the season, but she'd carried on wearing them anyway.

'Thank you.'

'Would you like to sit down?'

She smiled, and walked to the settee. 'This is a nice place.'

'It's great, isn't it? I have a really great estate agent.'

Becca smiled. 'You should introduce me some time.'

'Would you like a drink?'

'Thanks.'

'Coffee? Tea?'

'Coffee, thanks. Black.'

Becca reached down and fiddled with the back of her shoe,

suddenly feeling terribly grown-up. Then before she fully realised what she was doing she'd found she'd unbuckled them and taken them off. She looked down at her toes and started laughing.

'What's funny?' he called from the kitchen.

'I don't know. You complimented my shoes and I took them off.'

He walked in from the kitchen. 'I really like your top.'

She laughed again and stood up. Then she raised her arms and took off the light green top she was wearing. Chris was smiling at her.

'Wow,' he said, 'cool game.'

Becca looked at him. 'I like your smile.'

He frowned. 'Does that work?'

'Just about.'

'Just don't say you like my eyes.'

'Why not?'

'Because I don't think I can bring myself to pop them out.'

'Ugh,' she said, 'you could just close them.'

'Right,' he laughed, 'the easy option. Still want your coffee?'

'Come here.'

She liked the little moment of indecision as he stood there, looked at her, and then looked back at the kitchen. Becca relaxed against the arm of the settee. Chris sat down beside her.

'Is what I think's going to happen going to happen?'

'Would you like it to?'

'I'd like it very much.'

'Good,' she said. Becca started kissing Chris, untucking the back of his shirt and putting her hand on his back.

He wriggled away, and said, 'I know this is going to sound weird, but do you mind if we don't do this here.'

'You want to go to a hotel?'

'No, I just mean, not here, on this settee.'

She looked at him. He seemed embarrassed. She could tell he hadn't wanted to say this, and sensed that he was still worried he might screw things up. But Becca loved dates like this. Odd preoccupations, after all, had drawn her to almost all her previous boyfriends.

'Is the bedroom OK?'

'Of course.' He paused. 'Are you sure you don't want your coffee?'

'It's fine,' she said. 'Unless you're desperate for some?'

'Oh no,' he replied. 'I don't even like the stuff that much.'

She laughed, and stood up. 'Is it through here?'

'That's right.'

'Wow,' she said.

'What?'

'Great poster.'

'Do you like it? I took the place because of that. It's really weird. I don't know why she didn't want it.'

'Who?'

'The woman who owns this flat.'

'Do you know her?'

'Oh no, she's very mysterious. I've only ever met Jessica.'

'Your estate agent.'

'Right.' He lay down on the bed, fully clothed. She joined him. They faced each other. He wrapped his arms around her.

'OK?' he asked.

'Yes,' she said, 'I like it here.'

'Good.'

'It feels safe.'

'In my arms, or in the flat?'

'Both.'

'If this was a film . . .' Chris began.

'All life is a film, you know that.'

'Right. But which film is it?'

'What?' she said, wondering if he'd twigged. 'You mean just this moment now?'

'Yes.'

'That depends. What do you want it to be? *Last Tango in Paris*?'

'God, no.'

'How about *Falling in Love*?'

'Hmmm, that sounds nice. You're Meryl Streep and I'm Robert De Niro. But who's Harvey Keitel?'

'Scarlett.'

He laughed. 'You're terrible.'

'So are you.'

'When I was younger, I used to think it was really sophisticated to fancy Meryl Streep.'

'Why?'

'I don't know. She seemed different then. All actresses seemed different then. Like Jessica Lange. Or Diane Keaton.'

'Anjelica Huston.'

'Exactly.'

'Film stars aren't usually that fanciable really, are they?'

'I know what you mean.'

'It's partly to do with all that lying. You know, short men pretending to be tall, adulterers playing at being happily married, gay people pretending to be straight.'

'Twentysomethings playing teenagers.'

'Yeah, although I always feel envious of those guys. It must be like reliving your adolescence all over again.' She rubbed her left eye. 'Have you ever seen a film star you fancied?'

'What? In real life?'

'Yeah.'

'I saw Parker Posey in a newsagent's once.'

'Does she live over here?'

'I don't know. I think she used to. With some English actor.'

'Who?'

'Stuart Townsend. He was in *Wonderland* and *Shooting Fish*.'

'Right.'

Chris smiled. 'What are we doing?'

'Pardon?'

'What are we doing?' he repeated.

'What do you mean?'

'I mean, here we are in bed together for the first time and we're talking about Stuart Townsend.'

She smiled. 'It's nice.'

'It is, isn't it? But where do we go from here?'

'What d'you mean?'

'Well, my mind's racing, and I want to talk to you all night. But I also want to have sex with you. Very badly.'

'I feel exactly the same way.'

'So . . .'

'So, kiss me again. And when it's over we can go back to Stuart Townsend.'

'I've got something to tell you,' Chris said to Andy as they walked downstairs to the bar in the Curzon Soho.

'OK,' said Andy.

'I slept with Becca.'

'At fucking last. How long have you been chasing that woman?'

'It's been difficult. She feels guilty about her boyfriend. I guess that sounds stupid to you.'

'Why do you say that?'

'I don't know. I guess because you don't worry about stuff like that.'

'What d'you mean? Why don't I worry about stuff like that?'

'Because it's easier for you to persuade women into bed. You're more confident.'

'Well, I don't know what gives you that idea, but if you want me to prove I understand what you're talking about, let me tell you a story.'

'OK, but I think I need a beer first.'

'Don't worry, I'm about to get you one. Go find us a seat.'

Andy walked up to the bar. Chris sat next to one of the pillars pasted with the facsimiles of old Hollywood scripts. He looked at the photographs and words curling round the sides and smiled as he read a section from *Glengarry Glen Ross*. He really liked the Curzon, although he hadn't taken to it with quite the gusto that most of his cineaste friends had, still preferring the more laid-back, urban feel of the Metro. There was something worthy about the Curzon that put him off. It was nice to have a good art-house cinema in the centre of the city, and whenever a decent French film came out, he always headed there as his first choice, but he had never really seen anything surprising at that cinema, nothing quite as illicit and entertaining as the riskier stuff he had enjoyed at the Metro.

Andy returned with the beers. 'OK, I'm a bit embarrassed to tell you this because I have to admit that my actions in this story were influenced by a film that you think is amazing and I think is shit.'

'Which film?'

'What's your favourite Polanski movie?'

'*Bitter Moon*?'

'That's the one. You remember that bit at the beginning when Peter Coyote sees Emmanuelle Seigner on the bus and gets all fixated about her and can't stop thinking about her until he sees her in a shop window?'

'Yeah.'

'Well, there was a woman, about six months ago, and the same thing happened to me. It was a book shop, stupidly enough. She wasn't my usual type . . . you know I haven't got a fetish for those studenty women, but she was just, I don't know, there was something about her that made me feel, for one of the first times ever, that maybe it would be perfect to meet one woman and fall in love with her and stay with her for ever . . . she looked like, if you were with her, then you'd feel like you got everything right.'

Chris's voice was quiet as he sipped his pint. 'That's how I feel about Becca.'

'See, I knew you knew what I meant. Anyway, the first time I saw her I didn't say anything. I just bought some terribly pretentious book and tried to look all serious and bookish as I took it up to the till. And I carried on like that for a fortnight, until all the guys on the show thought I was trying to reinvent myself as some sort of arty, intellectual film critic, and I had to admit to them what was going on. Of course, they gave me all the usual advice, seize the day, go for it, ask her out. So the next day, I do it, and she says yes, straight away, and I feel really stupid, unable to believe I wasted so much time. And I go to work on fucking cloud nine, every film I review that day gets a five-star review. Then, that night, she phones me and says she's really sorry but she can't go on a date with me. So I ask her why and she says she's got a boyfriend and she didn't think it mattered but now she realises that, yes, it does matter, and because of that she can't go out with me.'

'That's awful. Why do all your stories have such unhappy endings?'

'Do you think that's an unhappy ending?'

'Isn't it?'

'No.'

'Why not?'

'Because that made her all the more perfect. If it hadn't mattered to her, it wouldn't have been worth it.'

Chris considered this.

'So what's your long-term plan?' Andy asked.

'I don't know. I'm not sure I have one.'

'And when are you seeing her next?'

'I don't know. She said she'd phone.'

'And will she?'

'Oh yeah, I'm sure. I don't want to brag or anything, but it was pretty incredible.'

'Illicit sex always is.'

'It's not just the sex. It's her. She talks the same way we do, you know, half bullshitting and half being serious, but always prepared to argue every point as if it was of life-or-death importance. And she's interesting without being kooky. That's what's so amazing about this girl ... she likes weird stuff without being, y'know, weird.'

Andy laughed. 'She sounds perfect for you.'

'She is.'

'Then why don't you ask her to leave her boyfriend?'

'I don't know if that's what I want. Perhaps I'm not supposed to have a relationship with this woman. Perhaps we're only supposed to have the most wonderful affair.'

'Do you believe that?'

'No.'

'Then ask her.'

'I slept with Chris.'

'That's great.'

'No, it's terrible.'

'Why? What did he do?'

'Oh no, it was perfect. It was everything I'd hoped for. That's why it was terrible.'

'OK, I hope you realise you're going to have to give me details.'

Becca cradled the phone beneath her chin as she used the remote to turn down the television. 'Scarlett, I can't ... I'm crap at that sort of thing.'

'Come on, you needn't think I gave you all that help for nothing. I've always wondered what Chris was like. Not that he's ever shown any interest in me.'

'You don't fancy Chris, do you?'

'Nah, Andy's more my type ... although he's always been more interested in my friends. But I'm curious about both of them. And now I have this opportunity to get some first-hand information.'

'Really, Scarlett, I'm going to disappoint you. You know how other girls can describe all kinds of details without getting embarrassed?'

'Yeah.'

'Well, I'm not like that. It took all morning to work up the courage to tell you I'd gone to bed with him.'

'I'm not asking for intimate details. Just give me a broad overview.'

'I feel self-conscious. No one's ever asked me this sort of thing before.'

'No one's ever asked?'

'Well, apart from Diana, and that's just 'cause she only met me a couple of times. My other friends know what I'm like. And no one's ever been interested in what it's like to sleep with James.'

'OK, I'll ask you questions. Was he romantic?'

'Yeah, I suppose so. Not in a candlelight-and-flowers sort of way. He didn't say anything stupid.'

Scarlett giggled. 'Is that what usually happens?'

'Oh, God, see, I told you I wasn't any good at this. Yes, most of my previous first times have been spoilt when my boy-friend's said something stupid.'

'But Chris didn't do that?'

'No. I was worried because before it happened, when we were lying in bed together, we were talking about films . . . and I thought that after it was over he might make some joke or reference that would belittle the experience.'

'So what did you talk about afterwards?'

'Oh, no, we did talk about films, but in a nice way.'

'And you didn't mind that?'

'No . . . I preferred that. It seemed safe. The worst thing would've been if he'd asked about whether the sex meant anything . . . if he'd gone on about us having a future.'

'Why? Don't you?'

'I don't think so.'

'But I don't understand. You got together, had fantastic sex, and now you're going to finish it?'

'I'm no good at affairs, Scarlett. If this carries on, I'm just going to get depressed about the state of my life.'

'What d'you mean?'

'I mean, I'm out of work, I'm screwing up the first relationship I've had that's felt like a step forward, and I'm beginning to wonder if I'm incapable of growing up.'

'But what's this got to do with Chris?'

'It's got nothing to do with Chris. That's why I don't want to expose him to it. Look, I know it sounds irrational. I know I'm contradicting myself. But this isn't the right time for me to get together with someone new. And there's more to it than that. When I went out for a drink with Diana, she told me things had never worked out between her and Chris because he fell in love with her at the wrong time. I can't put Chris through all that again.'

'But, Becca, none of what you're saying sounds particularly serious. And I'm sure Chris would rather you tried to work through all this with him than break off the relationship.'

Becca looked at the wall. 'I know Chris is your friend, Scarlett. And I am grateful. For everything. But I can't go out with him just because you think it's a good idea.'

Scarlett didn't reply.

'I'm sorry,' Becca said quickly, 'that was rude. I don't know why I said that.'

'It's OK,' Scarlett answered. 'I've made you feel defensive. It's my fault, I get too interested in other people's affairs. It's because I'm not working. But, listen, before I go, promise me one thing.'

'OK.'

'Just think seriously before getting rid of Chris. He's a good man, and he thinks the world of you.'

Becca said goodbye and hung up, wanting to get off the phone before she started crying. She felt so stupid, wondering why she was making such a mess of this. Most people had affairs all the time and didn't get screwed up by them. And this was a nice affair, arranged only to her benefit. So far, she'd controlled the whole thing, and didn't have to worry about waiting by the phone, or whether there was another woman, or anything. And Chris had been spectacularly nice, not putting the pressure on or calling her bluff by pretending there were other women in his life. So why was she so worried about seeing him tomorrow, and why couldn't she bring herself to enjoy what was happening? She wished she could've told Scarlett her secret, knowing she would be able to put it into perspective.

She didn't know why it seemed so important. Because it wasn't Scarlett-sanctioned probably. It was fine to tell Chris that she'd got drunk and tried to replicate a scene in *Working Girl* because that hadn't been her idea. But to tell him that before all this, before they'd even met each other, she'd sneaked into his house and gone through his stuff somehow wasn't OK. And she knew she wouldn't be able to keep quiet about it forever. At some point in the future, probably just after she'd ended her relationship with James, it would all slip out and he'd decide she was a weirdo and call everything off.

Becca turned the volume back up and flipped through the channels until she found something she could face watching, staying slumped on the sofa for the rest of the afternoon.

Chris sat down at his desk. Eating a biscuit, he looked through his completed pages and felt an unusual sense of satisfaction. With everything else he had written, it hadn't been until he'd seen it in print that it seemed even halfway competent. This time, however, he genuinely believed that he'd produced something worthwhile. He still wasn't sure who would want to publish it, or even if he'd be able to sell it, as it was only really a record of his personal reaction to romantic films rather than anything more thoroughly thought out, but at least he was close to completing something he felt proud of.

It'd started raining outside. Chris rubbed his eyes and checked his small black Tristar clock. Seven-thirty. He'd decided to treat himself to dinner at the nearby Italian restaurant where he'd taken Becca on their first proper date. He was partly allowing himself a meal out because the book was going so well, and partly because he was in a good mood because Becca was coming over tomorrow.

Chris placed his clock on top of the piled pages, and took his jacket from the back of the chair. He checked his pockets for his keys and switch card, then headed out into the rain.

Becca gave her hair one final brush, picked up her bag from the bed and left the house. She was late so she walked straight to the tube and ran down the escalator to catch the first train that came into the station. Once on the train she found a space away from the other passengers and allowed herself to spread out, putting her bag on the seat next to her and resting her feet on the seat opposite. She was wearing the blue sandals Chris had complimented her on during her last visit, thinking that if he liked them so much he deserved to see them again. Becca almost wanted to give them to him, wondering if he'd understand their relationship was over from this cryptic gesture.

She'd been in two minds about coming today. At first she thought she'd end their game with a scene from another of her favourite movies, *New York, New York,* but for that to work properly she should have arranged to meet him somewhere, and she didn't have the heart to pull another public no-show. So now she was going over, knowing it was the last time but not wanting to tell him, at least until the end of their afternoon together.

When the train reached the right station she took the lift to ground level and joined the queue at the ticket-barriers. Once through, she left the station and looked at her watch. She was almost thirty minutes late. No doubt Chris would be waiting at his window, taking great care to make sure he wasn't visible from the street.

Becca came up to her former local. Suddenly it didn't matter that she was late. She slipped into the pub, ordered a vodka tonic from the white-haired bartender, finished it in three large swallows and walked back out into the street.

She continued to Chris's place, then stood by the door and pressed the buzzer. Becca heard it sound inside and waited for Chris to appear. After a few seconds, she thought she could hear him coming down the stairs, but then the door didn't open. She buzzed again. And waited. Nothing. She buzzed three more times, and then heard noises inside again.

The door opened. A man in a mustard cardigan peered at her.

'Yes?' he asked.

'I'm here to see Chris. He knows I'm coming. I guess he's probably in the bath or something.'

The man nodded and stood back. She walked past him and up the stairs. She stopped outside Chris's door and knocked on it three times. Again, no response. OK, so she was late, but that was no reason for him to ignore her. Annoyed, she rapped again, this time so loud that there was no way he wouldn't be able to hear. A door opened opposite.

'I think he just went out, love. About five minutes ago.'

Becca looked at the woman telling her this. She nodded, and the woman retreated inside. She wished she hadn't knocked at all, and had instead just used her key to sneak inside. No doubt he'd have a shock when he returned, but that'd be the film star thing to do. And then when he returned they'd have a big row, and she'd explain everything. And it would all be sorted.

She took the key out of her bag.

And then put it back.

It was no good. She couldn't do it. But she did still have the urge to do something dramatic. She looked down at her feet, and the answer came to her.

Chris returned from Sainsbury's and let himself in. He walked upstairs, expecting to see Becca sitting there waiting for him. There was no sign of her. Well, that was fine too. He wondered if she'd shown up and gone, or if she just hadn't come at all, like the day in Bar Italia. Then he noticed the shoes.

It was her blue sandals. He picked them up and tucked them on top of his shopping. Then he unlocked the door and carried the bags through to the kitchen. He took out the shoes and placed them on top of the counter while he put the shopping away. Once that was done, he carried the shoes back into the lounge and put them on the coffee table.

Then he picked up the phone and called Scarlett.

'Hi, Chris, what's up?'

'I need a favour.'

'OK, what is it?'

'I need you to talk to Becca.'

Getting home had been hard. Every passing shoe seemed to want to stamp on her toes, and she overheard several unkind comments. It was only the fact that it was the wrong season that made her seem weird, although unfortunately Becca wasn't the kind of woman who'd go barefoot in summer and didn't even have that sense-memory to stop her feeling awkward.

When she got back, she noticed the number *3* flashing on her ansaphone. She played the messages. The first was from her mother, the second from James. And the third was from Scarlett.

'Hi, Becca, it's Scarlett here. Can you call me, please?'

Becca looked down at the ansaphone, feeling suspicious. She knew it was a bad idea to call her back, but she couldn't stop her finger dialling the number.

'Hi, Becca. Did you leave them yourself, or get someone else to go round?'

'What?'

'Your shoes. I just had a phone call from a very confused friend of yours.'

Becca sat on the carpet. She held the receiver under her chin while she tried to check the soles of her feet. They were very black.

'Oh, God.'

'So that time before, when we talked about this and you said you were breaking up with Chris, I guess that didn't happen, right?'

196

'I couldn't do it face to face.'

'So you just left him your shoes?'

'Yes.'

'Why?'

'I don't know. I'm confused.'

'I see. Well, don't you think you should at least call the poor boy and let him know your decision?'

'I can't,' she said.

'I see. Well, would you have any objection if I did it for you? I think he at least deserves that much.'

Becca didn't say anything.

'Shall I take that as a yes?'

'OK,' Becca mumbled.

'What was that?'

'I said OK.'

'Good.'

Chris picked up the phone the moment it rang.

'Scarlett.'

'No, Chris, it's me. Guess what?'

'What?'

Andy's brother paused before springing his momentous news. 'I've got an agent. He read the screenplay and he loves it, and he thinks he can get someone from Miramax interested in it.'

'That's fantastic,' Chris replied, wearily. 'How did it happen? Did you send the screenplay off?'

'No, I didn't want to risk that, so I just drove round some agents' offices, William Morris, The Agency, places like that, and I kept going until I found someone who was prepared to read it while I waited in reception.'

'And that's who liked it? William Morris?'

'No, they told me to fuck off. Well, they didn't put it like that, but that was what they meant. But I'm not worried, the agent I'm going to go with told me that William Morris wouldn't have known what to do with me.'

'And who is it you're going with? What's the company's name?'

'It's the Lucy Kable Agency, have you heard of them?'

'No, but like I told you, I don't really know anything about film agents.'

'The guy who's going to be representing me is called Julian Trench.'

'That's great.'

'What, his name?'

'No, that you've got representation.'

'I know.'

'So are you going to tell Andy now?'

'No, I'm going to wait to see if anything happens with Miramax first.'

'That's really exciting. But would you mind if I call you back later? It's just that I'm expecting a call.'

'No, no, that's OK, Chris, I understand. I only called to share my good news. You're the only person I've told, you see.'

Chris felt guilty. 'Well, I feel very privileged. Just remember to mention my name in your Oscar speech, OK?'

'OK, Chris. Bye.'

He hung up, then tried Scarlett's number. Engaged. He wondered if she was still talking to Becca. He hated having to do everything like this. But if this was how she wanted it.

The phone rang.

'Scarlett?'

'Hi, Chris, I've spoken to her.'

'And?'

'And I don't know what's going on. She won't tell me anything. She won't tell me why she's breaking up with you. Why she left the shoes. Anything. All she keeps saying is that she feels confused.'

'Maybe I should call her.'

'No, I don't think so. That was the one thing she was clear about.'

Chris sighed. 'So that's really it?'

'I think so. She said she was going to break up with you before.'

'Why didn't you tell me?'

'It was only a day or so ago. And I thought she might change her mind. Or, at the very least, I expected her to tell you herself. But she said it was too hard to do it face to face.'

'Why?'

'Probably because she knows she loves you.'

Becca had hardly been out since breaking things off with Chris. Instead, she stayed at home and watched *The Man Who Fell to Earth*, a film that she now felt she understood better than anything else she'd ever seen. All of the movie's riddles had resolved themselves to her, and she felt in complete sync with the film's sense of displaced longing.

It'd been hard not to let James see how she was feeling. For the first few days after the end of their affair, she felt so resentful towards her boyfriend that she could hardly bear to share the same bed. But gradually she had accepted that it was nothing to do with him and they had started to make love again, although James continued to handle her body with the careful wariness he had begun to show in recent months.

Today, however, she had decided that it was time to end her mourning. On the day after she had agreed to let Scarlett call Chris and tell him that she wouldn't be seeing him again, she had gone into town and headed to HMV, intending to buy copies of all the films that she and Chris had talked about while they were together. But after buying a copy of *The Breakfast Club*, she burst into tears and headed home. She hadn't realised at the time, but now she knew that the reason for her misery was that she was going against the relationship break-up routine that she had followed ever since her adolescence. What she needed to do was not to remind herself of Chris, but to set about trying to forget him. She wasn't one to wallow, never had been, and it made no sense to start now.

No, today she was going to HMV to remind herself that she

didn't need Chris to be happy. It had been extremely dangerous to go out with a man who was as interested in film as she was, and she was lucky that things hadn't gone any further. After all, if she'd gone out with Chris for a year, every film she thought about would remind her of him, and she would lose the sanctuary she'd always claimed as her own.

She dressed and left the house, then caught the tube to Leicester Square. On the way there she began to wonder whether it was sad that she led such a limited life, and could only seek changes by buying CDs and videos. Maybe this was all wrong. Maybe what she needed was not a new set of tapes, but a holiday. James would probably be delighted to take her somewhere, and although she would probably be fidgety for the first couple of days, it wouldn't take her long to relax into it. They hadn't managed to go anywhere this summer, and although she hadn't been concerned about this because she'd been working, maybe the strain was starting to show.

She went into the record store, walked through the first floor, stopping briefly at the sale videos at the front, and then continued to the larger selection upstairs. She had picked up a basket, and was intending to spend at least a hundred pounds. It was coming straight out of the rent money Chris had paid to her through Jessica, so there seemed a neat justice in this.

She started off with a copy of *Chasing Amy*. She'd always thought of Kevin Smith as one of 'her' directors, and although they hadn't talked about it, she had a fairly strong suspicion that Chris didn't rate his films. Pleased with this choice, she decided to go for the whole NJ trilogy, adding *Clerks* and *Mallrats* to her basket. Feeling lucky, she went to the front of the shop and was amazed to find an ex-rental copy of *Dogma*. Then she walked back and picked up both Austin Powers movies. Still feeling in the mood for those sort of light, bubbly teenage films, she picked up copies of *Nowhere* and *The Doom*

Generation. Worried she might get sick of teen movies, she had a look round for something serious. There was a copy of *The Onion Field* for five ninety-nine so she picked that up too, then looked to see if they had a copy of *Out of the Blue*. They didn't have that so she took *Paris Trout* instead, even though she wasn't sure if she could bring herself to watch it again. She decided that after she had got so much consolation out of *The Man Who Fell to Earth*, she should go for another couple of Roeg films, so she bought *Eureka* and *Castaway*, even though she had a feeling she would regret the latter. Then, an impetuous mood overtaking her, she added *Bad Timing* and headed up to the till.

Chris watched Becca come out of HMV with her two carrier bags full of videos. He was curious to know what she'd bought, and wondered whether her choices had anything to do with him. He decided she had probably bought the few films they'd talked about that he'd seen and she hadn't. He let her get as far as the street artists in Leicester Square, then crossed and started following her.

He followed her as far as the tube, then realised his pursuit was futile. He waited ten minutes then headed into the tube himself and made his way home.

As soon as he got back, he went upstairs, unlocked his door, walked through to the bathroom and started running a bath. He had his class that evening, and although he would give anything to be able to cancel it, he didn't want to disappoint his students and knew that if he didn't go, he'd just lie around the flat not doing anything. Walking back into his lounge, he picked up a TV and radio supplement and took it into the bathroom. He sat on the toilet and flipped through it, looking to see if there was anything worth watching when he got back.

There was nothing really. *The Lonely Guy* was on BBC 2 at 12.15, but he had it on video and there was no real reason to stay up late for it. Oh well. Maybe he'd feel like working on his book after a bit of intellectual fencing with his students. They seemed to be getting much more combative recently, which he suspected was because he was becoming more belligerent. He'd gone from feeling reluctant about sharing his opinions to insisting that everyone had to come up with forceful reasons for disagreeing with him.

He watched the bath filling and wondered what would stop him feeling sorry for himself. Watching so many romantic movies recently had made him forget the fact that love for him rarely happened in that straightforward way. He did believe in love at first sight, but even then his heart always needed a little push. But with Becca, the story was even more subtle. It was like the first forty minutes of *Short Cuts* where the story gradually creeps up on you and to begin with you're not sure whether you're going to stay or go and then by the time you've made up your mind it's too late and there's no way you can leave. Then when you get to the ending you feel dissatisfied and sit there until the credits have finished rolling, just in case there's a little extra explanation at the end. And when that fails to materialise, you're forced to re-examine what you have got, to go back over the movie until you realise that all the explanations are there, you just didn't notice them at the time, and now you'll have to go back and see the film again. This was Chris's favourite type of movie, films that infected his mind and left him worlds that he would slip into during his sleep.

After his bath, Chris dried himself and went into the bedroom to dress for his class. He felt depressed that he hadn't done more to prepare, especially as he'd wasted most of the week moping. It wouldn't be so bad if he'd scheduled a screening and could hide at the back, but unfortunately this was down as a discussion lesson. He considered springing a surprise movie on them, but couldn't think of anything he felt like watching. Besides, it was getting close to the end of term, and attendance always began to slip with the approach of Christmas. With any luck, he'd be facing a near-empty classroom.

He wasn't that worried. It was fairly easy to kill time in class, and if the worst came to the worst, he could always say something provocative about Hitchcock and let the old men argue it out for the rest of the lesson.

Chris's Favourite Films #23

The King of New York

Something weird happened to Chris when he went to watch Abel Ferrara films. Everything he usually hated in films suddenly became his favourite thing. Guns, cops, macho male actors. It all worked perfectly. *The King of New York* wasn't his favourite Ferrara film – that honour went to *The Blackout* – but it was the one he always pulled out to convince Ferrara virgins that they had something new to do with their lives.

Walken was incredible, of course, as he always was. Chris thought this was probably his best performance, if not quite as amusing as his role in the film version of *The Comfort of Strangers*. But it was the wonderful look of the film, and the sneaky way it attempted to convince you a life of coke 'n' whoring might be fun after all. Chris knew this wasn't true, but for the hundred or so minutes it took the film to run, he did always find himself wistfully longing for a change of career.

Most people liked the grime of Ferrara's films, but Chris liked the gloss. It was like an extended hip-hop video, a perfect film to watch with one finger on fast-forward. Andy hated Ferrara – even *Bad Lieutenant* – and couldn't understand why Chris rated him so highly. This made Chris like Ferrara's films even more.

Becca sat at their dining-table, waiting for James to bring in her dinner. She was pleased that he was cooking for her, but didn't understand why he was making such a big deal out of it. OK, so he hadn't pampered her in a while, but it hadn't been that long, and he usually made a point of deliberately not making a fuss when he was being nice, as if to rebuke her for the performance she put on whenever she was spoiling him.

He nipped through from the kitchen, took a box of matches from his shirt pocket, and lit the candles.

'Let me see those matches again,' she said.

'Why?'

'They're distinctive. Come on.'

He hesitated, then handed them over.

'Nice. Are they from a club?'

'I don't know. I think I stole them from someone at work.'

She looked at him, wondering why he looked so shifty. 'So you haven't been on another date with Diana?'

'No, and it wasn't a date anyway, it was just lunch.'

'Which time?'

'The only time.'

She tossed the matches back. 'OK.'

'I do work in Soho, you know. I don't have to go on dates with actresses just to get trendy matches.'

She laughed. 'OK, I'm convinced.'

He laced his arms around her and gave her a squeeze. 'Good. Now go and open the wine.'

Chris sat in the nook of The Black Pussycat, having unwisely accepted an invitation to join his students for a pint. He'd expected them to stop trying to get him out after he'd turned them down for the last three weeks running, but clearly they were impossible to offend.

He always felt awkward when he was out with his class, worried he would lose what little authority he had if he drank too much or said something stupid. He'd tried to talk about these feelings with the other teachers at the Lomax Centre, but soon realised that most of his colleagues relied on their classes for much of their social life.

His favourite student was here tonight, sitting two spaces up on the other side of the table. He liked Nadine because she so clearly liked him, and took such trouble to agree with everything he said in class. And when he said something so outrageous that she'd look stupidly fawning if she agreed with him, she was so deferential in her disagreement that it was even more flattering than when she said he was right.

Chris felt glad that Nadine was two spaces away. It was impossible to have an intimate conversation without drawing the attention of the rest of the class, and for that he was grateful. The last thing he needed to do tonight was go home with one of his students. Instead he was stuck with a small pack of serious movie-nuts, who had spent the last fifteen minutes trying to get him to name his all-time favourite actress.

'I don't know,' he said. 'Rosanna Arquette.'

'You're not serious,' said a blond boy who spent his days working on a building site. 'You can't still find her attractive after that bit in *Crash*?'

'I find her more attractive after that bit in *Crash*.'

'Her sister is so much sexier.'

'No way.'

Nadine looked over. 'I prefer her brother.'

'Which one?'

'Huh?'

'Alexis or David.'

'Who's Alexis?'

'You know, the weird one. He was in that film that Chris told us to watch when it was on TV.'

'No, not that one. I meant David. He's so sexy as Deputy Dewy. I think that's my favourite character in modern cinema.'

Chris looked at Nadine, wondering what the other students thought of her. He had been careful not to get too caught up in the romantic movements of his class, and although he had inevitably heard some gossip about his students, there had been nothing so far about Nadine.

'It's an interesting character,' Chris agreed, 'and I think it's interesting that Arquette is better in mainstream movies than art-house films. Did anyone see *Johns*?'

A couple of the movie-nuts nodded.

'Did you like it?'

'It was OK.'

'Sure, but it wasn't brilliant, right?'

'What about *Never Been Kissed*? He was crap in that.'

Chris remembered his all-nighter in the Prince Charles and tried not to get depressed. 'True. But I don't think that was his fault. I think most of the problems in that movie stem from the fact that Drew Barrymore produced it.'

'How d'you mean?'

'It's a vanity project. Probably the most gratuitous example of its kind since Duvall's *Apostle*.'

He stopped talking, aware that he'd taken on his teacherly tone and the students were now staring at him as if he was delivering an out-of-hours lesson. He also noticed that his glass was empty and thought this might serve as a good excuse to slip away.

'Another pint, Chris?' the blond boy offered.

'No thanks,' he said, standing up, 'although if there's any insomniacs among you, *The Lonely Guy* is on late tonight.'

He kissed the two women goodbye and shook hands with the half-dozen men who'd come along to the pub. It wasn't until he got outside that he started feeling like a twat. He thought of his students setting the video or staying up late, and wondered what part he was playing in these people's lives. All the other people he knew in the adult education profession were much more pragmatic about it, believing that if there were people who wanted to be taught, there was no shame in teaching them. Maybe if he had a more practical skill, like cooking or car maintenance, he would feel less concerned about taking their money for simply showing up once a week.

He walked away from the pub and made his way home.

He worked on his book for a bit, then went to bed. But finding it hard to sleep, he turned the light back on and went through to the lounge to watch TV. He thought of his students, then found *The Lonely Guy*. It had already started, but he'd seen it so many times that this didn't matter. Before long, the film reached the section where Steve Martin is jogging with a canister of fake sweat. Seeing a pretty girl in a coffee shop, he stops and goes inside. Stuck for a conversation-starter, he leans over and checks what she's reading. The book is . . .

The Mayor of Casterbridge.

Of course. That was why Becca had brought that book to the cinema with her. It was a reference to this film. But why had she chosen this particular scene? Did she think he was a lonely guy? And if she did, was that flattering or insulting? And how did she know that he would get the reference? Was she disappointed when he hadn't? And why hadn't she brought it up again since then?

He thought back to the times he had seen Becca, searching for clues to prove that she'd been acting out any other scenes. There was the day she didn't show. Perhaps that was a scene too. But from which movie? He couldn't think. What else? They had talked about their lives being like a movie just before they had first made love, and he had asked her what film she'd most like to be in. But she had already decided. He just hadn't picked up on it.

He looked back at the TV, wondering if there was anything else she had borrowed from this film. He watched it for another five minutes and then switched it off, unable to concentrate. He thought back to the first time they'd met. That had been a scene too, hadn't it? And he'd guessed it straight away. *True Romance*. But hadn't he been the one who'd brought it up? And didn't she seem surprised when he said it? Maybe he'd given her the idea to start setting up scenes. Fuck. He wanted this girl out of his head.

He turned the TV on again, then off, then picked up the phone. But who was he going to call at this time of night? Andy would probably be up, and Scarlett, but he doubted either of them would be that impressed. If only he had Becca's number. Then again, even if she had given it to him, would it have been much use? She was getting on with her life. The whole thing was a missed opportunity, and he would have to resign himself to that fact.

Becca let James undress her, enjoying the sensation of his hands against her skin. She had drunk heavily at dinner, and although she'd worried it would make her woozy, it didn't seem to be having that effect. Instead she was surprised to discover that she was actually looking forward to having him make love to her. The last few times she had felt like she was betraying Chris, but for the moment at least she had managed to put him out of her mind.

They stumbled across to the bed and Becca rolled backwards, allowing her boyfriend to tug at the legs of her jeans. She was giggling as he finally managed to get them off and she turned to see him sitting on the floor still fully dressed. He made a face at her, obviously unaware of how sinister he looked. Becca found she quite liked the strange new edge he was getting to his appearance. She'd never been an admirer of sideburns before, and had she not been too distracted by Chris to notice James growing them, she would've put a stop to them long before they reached their present state. But now that he had managed to sneak them by her, she had to admit that they were an interesting addition to his previously conservative appearance.

'Nice down there, is it?' she asked.

He threw the jeans to one side and jumped on the bed with her. Bouncing twice on the mattress, he pushed himself up on top of her body and started kissing her with aggressive enthusiasm. She pushed him up.

'What's got into you?'

'Nothing.'

She let him back into her arms. He pulled her black top up over her body and cupped her breasts from below. She let him touch her, and waited as he started kissing her again. Then he broke away to undress and switch off the light. Becca finished undressing in the darkness, then closed her eyes as James began to make his way up her body, those new sideburns surprisingly prickly against her thighs.

Chris was awoken at ten by an insistent buzzing. He got up and walked to the door, then continued down to the front of the house. Waiting outside was a man wearing a brown leather jacket and a grey fedora hat.

'Yes?' Chris asked, surprised by the man's appearance.

'Hi,' he said, shaking his hand, 'is Becca in?'

Chris pushed his hands into his jeans pockets, embarrassed about his bare chest.

'What?'

'Becca Coles. Brown hair, medium height, pretty.'

'What makes you think she lives here?'

'Oh, look, she probably doesn't any more. It's just, I know this sounds stupid, but it's been a couple of years, and she was the only person I thought was likely to stay put.'

Chris blinked at the stranger. 'Do you know who I am?'

'What?'

'You know I'm a friend of Becca's? Did she tell you to come here?'

'No, it's just, look, are you her new boyfriend, or something?'

'Why don't you come in?'

'If you're sure, mate. That'd be great. I'm Colin.'

'Hi, Colin, I'm Chris.'

Chris stood back and let Colin come inside. As he did so, Chris noticed how badly the man smelt. He was carrying a battered backpack, which was far too bright for the rest of his outfit. Some kind of traveller by the look of it. Chris led him upstairs and showed him inside.

'So you are Becca's boyfriend,' he said with assurance.

'Why do you keep saying that?'

'Well, you live with her for one.'

'Becca doesn't live here,' Chris almost shouted, unbelievably irritated by the man's unshakeable confidence. '*I* live here.'

'And she's moved out?'

'She was never here!'

Colin put his hands up, palms outward. He suddenly seemed very cautious, as if Chris was the nutcase.

'OK, you're right, she was never here. Do you mind if I sit down?'

'Help yourself.'

He made a big display of settling down, taking off his bag and coat, plumping up the cushions and then sinking back. Then he stared up at Chris, expectantly.

Chris sighed. 'Would you like something to drink?'

'That would be very nice. Thank you.'

'No problem. Tea, coffee, orange juice?'

'Coffee, thanks. Black, two sugars.'

Chris walked out to the kitchen. He carried the kettle to the sink, only just realising what was going on. It was another scene. Of course. He'd been stupid to think that things would finish so simply. Becca had clearly sent this man round to give him clues as to how to find her. He wasn't yet sure whether the man was a genuine friend or someone she had hired, but either way he was playing his part well. Chris made the coffee, poured an orange juice for himself and carried both mugs back into the lounge.

'OK,' said Chris, 'I'll play along. How do you know Becca?'

'We used to go out together.' He looked nervously at Chris. 'But don't worry, it was a long time ago.'

'And she sent you here?'

'No.'

'Oh, come on, you've done your bit. Now let's just jump to the end of the scene and you give me my clue. Like *3-2-1* only without the bin.'

Colin stared at Chris. 'Look, mate, I really think you're getting a bit confused. I don't know what happened between the two of you, but seriously, I'm not a part of it.'

'OK, we'll do it your way. So you're one of Becca's ex-boyfriends?'

'That's right.'

'But this was a long time ago?'

'Years.'

'And you've come here because . . .'

'Becca used to live here.'

'That's right. Becca used to live here. Would you like a bath?'

'Pardon?'

'I wondered if you'd like to use my bath.'

'Really? That would be fantastic, actually, thanks. I haven't had a chance to wash in at least two weeks. Are you sure you don't mind?'

'Not at all. And then maybe I could take you to lunch.'

Colin looked at Chris, suspicious again. But hunger seemed to get the better of him, and he said,

'That would be very Christian of you. Thank you very much.'

'No problem at all. I suppose you know where the bathroom is?'

'Yes,' he said. 'Shall I go now?'

'Why not?'

Chris waited until Colin was safely in the bathroom, then picked up the phone and dialled his estate agent. He felt vaguely disgusted that he could hear Colin filling the bath.

'Hi, Chris, what's up?' said Jessica as she came on the line.

'Are you busy?'

'It's not too bad. Why?'

'I just wondered if I could take you to lunch.'

Jessica hesitated. 'Any particular reason?'

'Not really. I just fancied a chat. And I've got someone I think you'd like to meet.'

'OK,' she said, 'I guess that'd be OK. Where did you have in mind?'

Colin's hair looked even more lank when he came out of the bathroom.

'Would you like to borrow my hair dryer?' Chris asked.

'No, I'd prefer to let it dry naturally.'

Chris looked at Colin, wondering if he could cope with eating with this man. Colin was wearing a dressing-gown that someone had given Chris as a present, and had been left hanging on the back of the bathroom door.

'So what type of food are we having?' Colin asked.

'Thai. Is that OK with you?'

'It's not my favourite.'

'I'm sorry to hear that.'

'But it's OK . . . I mean, I'll eat it.'

'Good.'

They arrived at the restaurant early. Colin was grumbling about how hungry he was so Chris let him order some starters. He was greedily tucking into these when Jessica came in. Chris spotted her and waved across.

'Hi, Chris,' she said, as she came to the table.

'Jessica,' he said, kissing her, 'this is Colin.'

Colin looked up from his food, his lips wet.

'Hello,' he said. 'I'd shake your hand but I've been eating with them.'

'That's fine,' she said, looking at Chris.

He handed her a menu. 'Colin came to my flat today.'

'Right,' she said, doubtfully, clearly waiting to see if it was a joke.

'He was looking for a woman called Becca.'

Jessica didn't say anything.

'Would you happen to know anyone called Becca?'

'Oh God,' she said, putting her head in her hands.

By the end of lunch, he had got it all out of her. She was surprisingly responsive, revealing all almost immediately. After hearing what she had to say, he promised he would not do anything to get her in trouble.

The only fact she didn't reveal was Becca's address. This was because after Colin had gone to the toilet, Chris had told her that he already had this information, and that he didn't want Colin to go round there. They spent the rest of the meal talking about how happy Becca was with her new boyfriend, and by the end of lunch Colin seemed to have got the picture, thanking Chris for the meal and ambling off in search of another ex-girlfriend who might be stupid enough to put him up. After he had gone, Jessica said,

'What a weirdo.'

'I know. Can you believe she used to go out with him?'

'Well, she did once tell me she had weird taste in men.' She laughed. 'Present company excluded.'

'So tell me more about what she said about me.'

'In complete confidence?'

'Of course,' he said. 'She'll never know.'

Becca was on the phone to James when the doorbell rang. She considered leaving it, expecting it'd probably be someone asking her about changing her gas to electric, or electric to gas. But then James told her to stop being stupid and go and answer the door.

'But you'll be back normal time tonight?'

'Yes. Now, hurry up, before they go away.'

'OK, OK, bye.'

She hung up and went to the door. It was Chris.

'Can I come in?'

'No.'

'Why?'

'I'm too scared.'

'About what?'

'That once I let you in, I won't be able to get rid of you.'

'Oh. Thanks.'

'No, I mean, I won't want to get rid of you.'

'That's better.' He paused. 'I think.'

She stepped back and let him inside.

'Where shall I go?' he asked.

'Through there.'

He went through to the living room.

'I met a friend of yours today,' Chris said.

'Who?'

'He was a bit dishevelled.'

'James?'

'No . . . he's just come back from a round-the-world trip.'

'Colin?'

'Well done. Would you like to guess where I met him?'

'Tell me.'

'He came to the house. Your house.'

'Oh,' she said, 'he told you.'

'I worked it out eventually. Although I realise I've been a bit slow on the uptake. About everything really.'

'What do you mean?' she asked, worrying he was about to launch into some elaborate emotional blackmail.

'The clues, the scenes . . . *The Lonely Guy*.'

'Oh, right, that. Well, that wasn't really your fault. I didn't get to do it properly with Scarlett being there.'

'But you did plan it?'

'Yes.'

'How did you know I'd be at the Metro?'

'Do you know the answer already?'

'No, why would I? Is it obvious?'

'That depends. I know you been talking to Scarlett. Have you spoken to anyone else?'

'Like who?'

'Jess, for example.'

'Did she call you?'

Becca laughed throatily. 'I knew it.'

'But she didn't tell me anything about that day.'

'Look, stay here, I need a drink if we're going to talk about this. Would you like something?'

'Do you have beer?'

Becca nodded and went to the kitchen. She returned with a bottle of white wine and a can of Red Stripe.

'Is this alright?'

Chris nodded. 'Fine, thanks.'

'I'm just going to come out and say it. Then you can decide how you feel about it and what you want to do.'

'Sounds fair.'

'I've been following you.'

'Right.'

'And I sneaked into your flat when you weren't there.'

'There are opportunities in this life for gaining knowledge and experience . . .'

'Exactly. I mean, it started like that . . . how much did Jessica tell you?'

'Nothing really. Just that it was your flat, and it used to belong to your aunt and that she'd spoken to you about me before we met.'

'Did she tell you how she described you?'

'No. Was it terrible?'

'No, not at all. I asked which celebrity you looked most like.'

'Who did she say?'

'David Duchovny.'

'Really? That's not so bad, is it?'

'No.'

'Usually when people compare me to film stars they always choose the ones who no one can remember. Like Timothy Hutton.'

'I can see that. I think Duchovny's more accurate, though.'

'Did she really say Duchovny? I knew I liked Jessica.'

'She's one of the nicest people I know. But look, Chris, this stuff is important. I don't want to talk about David Duchovny.'

'OK, OK, I'm listening. You broke into my flat.'

'Oh, don't put it like that. That sounds terrible. I sneaked in. I had a key.'

'Right.'

'Please, Chris, don't look like that. I didn't mean to, I mean the first time, it wasn't deliberate. You called Jessica and told her you wanted the keys to the French windows and I brought them across.'

'And you started exploring?'

Becca curled her legs up underneath her. 'When I saw your stuff, I just wanted to meet you. It wasn't because you had amazing stuff, or because you were into movies, or because a lot of those movies were the same ones I liked. It was just the feeling, of you in my space. It sounds ridiculous, but I thought you were the first person who fitted the flat since I'd left it. And I suppose I was also a bit envious of your life. Of your freedom. Of the fact that you had my flat and you were making a fresh start in it.

'Did Jessica tell you that?'

'What?'

'That I was making a fresh start?'

'She said you made jokes about being single. And that you had nice eyes.'

'Becca . . . why do you sound so sad?'

'Because I've realised how stupid I've been. I didn't mean to hurt you, Chris. I just wanted to have fun with you for a while.'

'And now it's over?'

'Yes.'

'Why?'

'Because it was never real. I made the whole thing up. I tricked you into having feelings for me.'

'You didn't trick me, Becca. And those feelings are real. Tell me about your relationship with James.'

'What do you want to know?'

'Are you happy with him?'

'I don't know.'

'Do you feel the same way towards him that you do towards me?'

'No.'

'Can I ask you a question?'

'Of course.'

'If it was the other way round . . . if you were living with me, and James was your tenant, and you were sneaking off from me to see him, would your feelings towards us be the same?'

'I don't understand the question.'

'What I want to know is, did this only happen because you're scared of getting older? Do you just feel nostalgic for your old life and scared of commitment? Or is this to do with me and him?'

Becca stared at Chris. 'I don't feel the same way towards James that I do towards you. But the feelings I do have for him, which at the moment are fairly negative, have been born out of our time together. They're genuine feelings. With you, I don't know. It's so much more exciting, and it feels like a real love affair, but that could only be because I've cheated. Who knows how things would be if we'd met and dated in the conventional manner.'

'So you're scared?'

'Yes.'

'Too scared to give up James?'

'What d'you mean?'

'If I got down on my knees and begged you not to finish things with me, but to leave James instead . . . to come with me and start the relationship again, to see if your flat really is magical and could make us fall in love for ever and ever, would you do it?'

'I don't know, Chris. I really don't know.'

The two of them sat there for a moment, exhausted by the emotional weight of everything that had been said.

'*The Lonely Guy*'s the only one I got, you know.'

'What?'

'The scenes. *The Lonely Guy*'s the only one I worked out, and I only got that one because it was on TV. Oh, and *True Romance*. With the popcorn.'

She smiled at him, her voice brightening. 'That wasn't deliberate. I was really nervous.'

'Really?' he asked. 'But there were others?'

She nodded. 'I thought you'd get *Wild Orchid* straight away.'

'*Wild Orchid*? What was that? Our first night in bed?'

'No,' she smiled, 'the game in the restaurant.'

'Do they play that in that film?'

She nodded. 'And me getting drunk in that bar was *Working Girl*. That was Scarlett's idea.'

'I don't mean to criticise, Becca, but these aren't exactly the most romantic choice of movies. What about *Brief Encounter, Gone With the Wind, Casablanca*?'

'Well, I did have some of those in mind. It's not my fault that you chose the scene from *Rocky*.'

'What scene from *Rocky*?'

'When I asked you to pick a colour. All the other scenes were really romantic. In fact, if you'd made the right choice you'd have been able to get into bed with me much earlier. But you chose the ice-skating scene from *Rocky*.'

'That was from *Rocky*? I figured it was from some seventies slush-fest. What about that day you stood me up? That was definitely a scene, wasn't it?'

'Yes, there you go. A perfectly conventional, normal, romantic scene.'

'Which film was it from?'

'*You've Got Mail*. Or you could've gone for the art-house version.'

'What was the art-house version?'

'Well, it was pretty impossible. I didn't hold out much hope of you getting this. Although it was re-released a few years ago.'

'Hang on ... let me guess.' He thought a moment. 'No, I don't know. Go on, tell me.'

'*La Maman et la Putain*.'

'Fucking hell, just a little bit obscure then.'

'Well, you had the mainstream option as well. It wasn't totally unfair.'

She leaned across and took Chris's hand. It didn't feel so bad now. She felt a bit embarrassed about the fuss she'd caused, and resolved to sort out the situation with dignity. It seemed impossible to continue with James, knowing she had someone like Chris waiting for her. She kissed him again, and then let him hold her for a while, trying to work out how she'd do what needed to be done.

'So how did you leave things?'

Chris wound the phone-cord round his fingers. 'What more could I say? I asked her to leave James and move in with me, and when she said she didn't know if she could, I told her to call when she'd made up her mind.'

'And she hasn't called?'

'No.'

'She might be trying now.'

'No, I've got call-waiting.'

Scarlett exhaled. 'I don't know, Chris, I wish I knew what to say. Did you tell her you'd met James?'

'No, I kept quiet about that. Do you think I should've said something?'

'Maybe. It sounds obvious that she feels guilty about following you. Letting her know that you've done your own share of espionage might help ease her mind.'

'But you told me to do it.'

'Oh yeah. Well, leave out that bit. Listen, Chris, I've got to go. Keep me informed, OK?'

'Of course.'

'And cheer up. I'm sure she'll come to the right decision.'

James was two hours late. Becca sat watching the television, waiting for him to apologise.

'I'm sorry,' he said. 'You haven't cooked anything, have you?'

'No.'

'Good. I was going to bring back some takeaway but I wasn't sure what you wanted.'

'James,' she said slowly, 'I know you hate it when I launch in on you the moment you get in from work, but we really need to talk.'

He looked at her. 'OK.'

'Do you want to get changed first?'

'If that's OK with you.'

She picked up the remote and lowered the volume of the TV. 'It's fine. Go and get changed.'

He put down his bag and walked through to the bedroom, hand going to the knot of his tie. Becca looked back at the television, then turned it off.

She hadn't planned what she was going to say. She'd been thinking about it since Chris had come round that afternoon, but had been unable to come up with anything beyond her opening sentence.

James returned and sat down opposite her, wearing a grey and white jumper that reminded her of her father.

'OK,' he said, 'what's up?'

'James, I don't know how to say this, but . . .'

'I think I know what you're going to say.'

She looked at him. 'Really?'

'You're not happy, are you?'

She started crying. 'I don't deserve you.'

'What are you talking about?'

'James . . . I've been cheating on you.'

'I know.'

'What?'

'I mean, I didn't know, but I had my suspicions.'

'Oh . . . and you're not furious.'

'God, I'm going to hate myself for this.'

'What?'

'This is so crap. What I should be doing is making you feel really guilty or flying off the handle. What I definitely shouldn't be doing is telling you that I've been cheating on you too.'

'What?' Becca asked, startled out of her misery. 'Who with?'

'You know who it is. You've asked me about her often enough.'

'Fucker,' she said, hitting him. 'You fucking fucker. I can't believe it.'

'Hang on, I bet you were unfaithful first.'

'That's got nothing to do with it. How could you go for her?'

'Is your new man so much better?'

Becca couldn't resist saying, 'Ask her.'

'What?'

'Nothing.' She wouldn't tell him. He'd find out soon enough. Although she couldn't help thinking back to the evening she'd spent with Diana. 'Look, what do you want to do?'

'I hadn't really thought about it. I take it the relationship's over.'

'You could say that.'

'Well, I'm not about to kick you out.'

'I don't want to live here any more.'

'You have somewhere to go?'

'Yes.'

'Your new man has a place or you have a place?'

'Somewhere between the two.'

'I see.' He coughed. 'You have been busy. So have you decided when you're going?'

'As soon as possible, I suppose. What about you?'

'Diana's only just left her boyfriend. She's not really ready to move in with me.'

'I see.'

'Don't be like that.'

'I'm sorry. You're right. So what now?'

He laughed. 'I don't know. Are you hungry?'

'Starving. My stomach's been playing up all afternoon, but now it feels fine.'

'Good,' he said. 'Then let's go and get a Chinese.'

'And a video.'

'For old times' sake?'

'Exactly.'

Becca's Dodgy Boyfriends #6
James

Becca met James when she was working on her travel programme *Run at the Sun*. He'd responded to an advert placed in
The Guardian by their researchers, asking for an ordinary bloke
in a normal earning bracket who worked so hard that he didn't
have time for a holiday. At first she wasn't all that interested in
him, thinking that he was attractive, but more the kind of man
her friends went out with. He told her early on that he was
single, but she didn't read anything into it, knowing that she
wouldn't be the sort of woman he was attracted to.

After she broke up with James, Becca found it hard to
remember what had attracted her to him. She supposed it was
his confidence, and his belief that he was a happy, successful
man. He didn't have any weird hang-ups, seemed unlikely to
experience anything so life-changing that she'd no longer have
a place in his life, and most importantly, seemed like someone
who would make a good husband and father. Even though he
betrayed her, she couldn't feel too badly towards him. Not just
because she'd been unfaithful too, but because the promises
they'd made each other had never really struck her as
completely sincere. They'd been playing at being grown-ups,
and she was merely grateful that it had all ended without
either of them getting hurt.

Andy sat down on Chris's sofa and cracked open a can of Stella.

'You know, Chris, I've got to tell you, I never liked Diana.'

'Really?'

'Only because she was an actress.'

'What's wrong with actresses?'

'They're always so needy. And you've got no idea whether you've got a good one. I mean, acting's a skill, and there are good actors and bad actors. But bad actors aren't actors who can't act as well as good actors, they're actors who can't act at all.'

'You're talking nonsense,' Chris told him.

Andy's brother laughed. 'I have to listen to him going on about stuff like this all the fucking time.'

'No, no,' protested Andy. 'What I'm saying makes perfect sense. Is Tom Cruise a better actor than Harrison Ford?'

'Yes.'

'No, what you mean is that you like Tom Cruise more than Harrison Ford. You can't explain to me why one is a better actor than the other.'

'So what's your point?'

'My point is that it's not like other disciplines. Did you know that the biggest factor in whether or not an actor gets a job is the quality of their voice?'

'Yes. Diana told me. They tell every actor that at drama school. I don't think it's true though. They only say that so the ugly kids don't get disheartened.'

Andy seemed to lose interest in his argument and looked across to the neat pile of paper stacked square on Chris's desk.

'What's that typescript?'

'My secret project. A week or so and it'll be finished.'

'I knew you were writing a novel.'

'It's not a novel.'

'What is it then? A study of somebody?'

'No, it's not a study. Well, it is, but not of one particular person.'

'Why are you being so secretive? You usually share all your ideas with me.'

'I know, but I told you before. This book is very personal. I don't want to let anyone see it until it's finished.'

Andy's brother sat up. 'What time did Becca say she'd be here?'

'Three. It's only five minutes past.'

The doorbell rang.

'There you go.'

Chris could tell Becca was nervous. When she entered the flat her eyes flicked over to the small wooden table on which he'd placed the pair of blue sandals she'd abandoned in the middle of their courtship. Then she looked at him as if surprised that he'd made a feature of this token, and he could tell from her slightly reproachful expression that she was upset he'd put out on display something that was supposed to be private.

'Are you OK?' he asked.

'Yes,' she said. 'I'm sorry. It just feels a bit weird. I've just had an odd conversation with James.'

'Oh,' he said, feeling slightly hurt. 'What sort of odd conversation?'

'I don't really want to talk about it.'

'Right.'

'Come on, Chris, you know what sort of conversation I mean. The final one.'

'How did you leave it? Never see each other again, or . . .'

'Oh, we'll see each other again. Socially, I mean. There wasn't enough passion in the relationship for it to really combust. Let's not talk about it now. Where's Andy?'

'In the other room.'

The journey over was fun, with the four of them quickly falling into friendly conversation. Andy didn't take long to draw Becca into film talk, and after that they happily dispensed with politeness, falling instead into a rhythm of taunt, compliment and insult that sustained them through a whole afternoon of hard physical labour. Chris reflected that this was the second time he had roped his friends into moving furniture and suspected it wouldn't be long before they called in the debt.

James, Becca told Chris, had agreed to be absent until evening and without this emotional entanglement the work was completed swiftly, leaving Andy's brother plenty of time to return the van. While he was doing this, Chris made everyone coffee. As he brought the cups in, he asked Andy,

'What are you doing Wednesday week?'

'Nothing. Why?'

'Scarlett's lot are showing their movie. It's not properly finished yet, but they're holding a special screening for friends and family. Do you fancy coming along?'

'Sure.'

'Great.'

Andy's brother returned from the van-hire place. Andy, Chris and Becca had finished their coffees, but Chris made everyone a second cup, to give Andy's brother the chance to drink a first. Chris's arms and shoulders ached as he sat down and from the way everyone else was sprawled around the flat he sensed they were also feeling the afterglow of warmed muscles.

'We'd better be going soon,' Andy said. 'We're having dinner with our parents.'

'OK,' said Chris. 'Thanks again for all your help.'

'Yeah,' added Becca, 'it was really kind of you.'

'Pleasure,' said Andy as he got to his feet. He walked over to where his brother was sprawled and tried to tug him up out of his armchair. 'Come on, you.'

'OK. Give me a minute. I haven't had as long to rest as you.'

Andy gave up and walked over to the window. 'It's a nice place, this.'

Chris looked to see if Becca was smiling. She wasn't. He reached out and took her hand.

Andy's brother got to his feet. 'OK, I'm ready now.'

'At last.'

Chris and Becca stood up. Andy kissed Becca and shook Chris's hand, patting him on the shoulder. Then his brother did the same, and they both left. Becca took this opportunity to move away from Chris, sitting in the place where Andy had been before.

'You OK?' he asked.

'Yes,' she said, 'just adjusting.'

'Does it feel weird?'

'A bit.'

Chris collected the coffee cups and took them out to the kitchen. When he came back, Becca was lying supine on the settee, staring at the ceiling.

'Did you know how this was going to work out?'

'No,' she said, 'I had no idea. Even when you came round and asked me to leave James, I still didn't know how it was going to end.'

'But you're pleased, right?'

She looked at him. 'Of course. I just want to get it all straight in my head.'

'What isn't straight?'

'Do you want me to talk about this?'

'Yes.'

'It's just, my life isn't the way I'd like it to be at the minute.'

'I understand.'

Becca stared at Chris, holding his gaze until he wasn't sure if he did understand after all. She sat up.

'I don't want to feel that I've got scared and stepped backwards into my past. I want to feel that I lost my way for a bit and now I've found it again.'

He kissed her. 'Can I tell you a secret?'

'Of course.'

'What do you think of Andy's brother?'

'He's nice. Why?'

'He's written a screenplay.'

'Really?'

'Yeah. It's about a baby that gets sent to Vietnam. It's utterly appalling, but somehow he's managed to get an agent and the agent's been telling him that he's going to sell the screenplay to Miramax.'

'That's great.'

'Yeah, except it obviously won't happen. And I just know he's going to be so disappointed.'

'How do you know he won't sell it?'

'I just have a feeling that Miramax aren't looking for a Vietnam baby comedy. But the thing is, he's made me promise not to tell his brother, and I'm desperate to break the promise, but I know that if I do he'll go mental.'

'So don't.'

'It all sounds so simple when you put it like that.'

'Let him have his dream. That way if he turns out to be

successful, he'll remember that you were the one who encouraged him. And if it doesn't work out, well, I'm sure the agent'll find a way of breaking it to him.'

'You're right.'

'I know. Come on, let's go for a drink.'

Chris's Favourite Films (New Entry)
Working Girl

After Becca had come clean to Chris about what she'd been up to, they spent a weekend indulging in a marathon viewing of all the films that had helped bring them together. They started with *The Lonely Guy* and *The Breakfast Club*, then watched *True Romance*, *Wild Orchid*, *Rocky*, *You've Got Mail* and then all four hours of *La Maman et la Putain*. But Chris's favourite of all the films was definitely *Working Girl*, a film he'd never properly appreciated first time round. The main reason why he'd never enjoyed it was that he found it hard to believe a film in which the heroine had chosen Harrison Ford (his least favourite actor) over Alec Baldwin (his favourite actor). But now that no longer mattered so much, and Becca responded by teasing him that wouldn't he rather have Joan Cusack than Melanie Griffith.

Chris had never had shared films in this way before. He had to admit that they were a strange bunch of films, but somehow if you put them all together he believed you did get the essence of his and Becca's relationship. Mainstream and arty, childish and mature, and at heart, probably a little too whimsical, he nevertheless felt proud of the combination.

They had both been scared about the screening. Mainly because they were both worried about running into their exes. Neither of them took much amusement from the fact that their previous partners had also hooked up, and weren't looking forward to what would be an inevitably awkward evening.

'I suppose we do have to go,' Becca said to Chris for about the twentieth time that afternoon. 'Scarlett will never forgive us if we don't.'

'Yes,' said Chris, 'but we could leave before the party afterwards.'

'That's a good idea. Would you be OK with that?'

'Of course,' he said. 'It's going to be awful. The film will be terrible, and everyone will be hovering round expectantly, waiting for us to praise them.'

'It will be awful, won't it?' said Becca, smiling.

Chris laughed. 'So do you know what the film's about?'

'Not really. Do you?'

He shook his head.

'Has Scarlett ever worked on anything good?'

'A few things. But I think our relationship was her most elaborate production to date.'

'How did you meet Scarlett?'

'Through Andy . . .'

'You're close, you and Andy.'

'We've been friends a long time. I'm surprised it's lasted. I'm a lot different than I used to be.'

'Different how?'

'I used to be a lot more ambitious.'

'But you're not now?'

'No.'

Becca laughed. 'So why have you just written a book?'

'I don't know. You, mainly.'

'What?'

'The book's not intended to be this fantastic work of criticism or anything like that. I started it because I was lonely, and then once I'd met you, I continued it because it was a way to carry on thinking about what was happening between us.'

'So why won't you let me read it?'

'I will do. Eventually. I just need to go over it one more time.'

The preview was at the Dalston Rio, a long way from their home. Andy's brother picked them up at seven. Andy was already sitting in the back of the taxi, flipping through a newspaper and folding it up as they climbed inside.

'Hi, guys,' he said, smiling.

'Hi.'

They didn't talk much during the journey, except to continue their speculation about whether the film would be any good. Becca repeated her observations about Joel, the scriptwriter, and Andy told them that Scarlett had called him in the middle of the night, panicking about the potential reception.

Scarlett was standing by the front entrance, next to the girl collecting invitations.

'Hi, Scarlett,' said Chris. 'Nervous?'

'God, yes,' she said. 'Mainly about what my parents are going to think.'

'The film's not that explicit, is it? It's only a fifteen.'

'Well, no, you don't see too much in it. But it is about voyeurism.'

Chris noticed James and Diana standing inside. Diana made a slight wave at him. Becca and James remained still. Chris kissed Scarlett on both cheeks, detached himself from Becca's arm, and walked across.

'Alright?' he asked.

She nodded. 'Actually, Chris, I've brought something for you. That's if you want it?'

He looked down and noticed the videotape in her hand.

'What is it? Some terrible film you picked up by mistake?'

'No, it's a tape of my TV show. You don't have to take it if you don't want to, but I thought you might like to see it.'

'Thanks,' he said, taking the tape.

He started to walk away. She called after him and he looked back.

'Yes?'

'Will you let me know what you think?'

'Of course.'

Scarlett stood in front of the screen, holding a microphone.

'Hi. Thank you all for coming. The director will be available for questions after the screening, but here to introduce the film is the screenwriter, Joel Conrad.'

Joel took the microphone. He was wearing his *Peep Show* T-shirt and heavy glasses.

'OK, right, yeah . . . um . . . what can I say? This is my baby. What's that? Sorry . . . right . . . our baby. I hope you enjoy it.'

Chris and Becca left the screening after the credits but before the questions. Andy winked at them and followed the couple out into the auditorium.

'You off?' he asked. 'Not staying for the party?'

'No, make our excuses for us, will you?'

'Sure thing. What did you think of the movie?'

Chris laughed. Becca joined in.

'Yeah,' said Andy, 'me too.'

'God, it was horrible, wasn't it?' said Chris, as they waited for a bus.

Becca nodded. 'One of the worst films I've ever seen. Poor Scarlett.'

'She'll bounce back. And who knows, maybe it'll pick up a cult following.'

Becca looked at him. 'What?'

He laughed. 'These things happen.'

The bus arrived. Becca got on. 'I bet you a thousand pounds it's dead in a week.'

Chris and Becca made love twice that night, before and after a two a.m. trip to the supermarket. After the second time, Becca dropped off while Chris remained awake. He felt distracted and restless, and after rolling over to check Becca was definitely asleep, he pulled back the duvet and walked through to the lounge.

Chris knew why he was awake. He had one last thing to do, a final exorcism. Fetching the tape Diana had given him, he turned the volume on the television down to a barely audible level and started watching the programme. It was better than he'd expected, certainly much more exciting than *Peep Show*. And although he did feel strange when he saw Diana on screen, he now knew this was something he could cope with. He had moved on, and felt happy with what had happened. Smiling to himself and shaking his head, he slid the tape in with the rest of their library and went to join Becca in bed.

Acknowledgements

Lesley Shaw, Neil Taylor, Christine Slenczka, Tibor Fischer, Simon Sheldrake, Sarah Ballard, Alexandra Heminsley, James Linville, Scarlett Thomas, Kate Le Vann, Nick Guyatt, Simon Trewin, Nicholas Blincoe, Leila Sansour, Lawrence Norfolk, Andrew Biswell, Huda Abuzeid, Bo Fowler, Sarah Waters, Sarah Harris, Candida Clark, Jim, Jamie and Catherine Shaw, Lana Citron, Stefan Marling, Jo Rideout, Jim Flint, Elaine Pyke, John Rush, Kaye, Dave and Louise Thorne.